Business Is Business 3

A Novel

Silk White

Good 2 Go Publishing

ISBN: 9781943686797
Copyright ©2016 Silk White
Published 2016 by Good2Go Publishing
7311 W. Glass Lane • Laveen, AZ 85339
www.good2gopublishing.com
twitter @good2gobooks
G2G@good2gopublishing.com
Faccbook.com/good2gopublishing
ThirdLane Marketing: Brian James
Brian@good2gopublishing.com
Cover design: Davida Baldwin
Interior Layout: Mychea, Inc

Printed in the U.S.A.

BOOKS BY THIS AUTHOR

10 Secrets to Publishing Success
Business Is Business
Business Is Business 2
Business Is Business 3
Married To Da Streets
Never Be The Same
Stranded
Sweet Pea's Tough Choices
Tears of a Hustler
Tears of a Hustler 2
Tears of a Hustler 3
Tears of a Hustler 4
Tears of a Hustler 5
Tears of a Hustler 6
Teflon Queen
Teflon Queen 2
Teflon Queen 3
Teflon Queen 4
Teflon Queen 5
The Serial Cheater
Time Is Money (An Anthony Stone Novel)
48 Hours to Die (An Anthony Stone Novel)

WEB SERIES
The Hand I Was Dealt Season 1
Episodes 1-8 Now Available Free On You Tube

The Hand I Was Dealt Season 2
Now Available

Acknowledgements

To all of you who are reading this, thank you for stepping inside the bookstore, stopping by the library, or downloading a copy of Business is Business 3. I hope you have enjoyed this read from top to bottom. My goal is to get better and better with each story. I want to thank everyone for all their love and support. It is definitely appreciated! Now without further ado Ladies and Gentleman, I give you *Business is Business 3*.

$iLK WHiTE

Business Is Business 3

Millie Mason

One

Millie stepped out of Mike's building with her head held high and a refreshed look on her face. One would never be able to tell that she had just murdered a man that she had raised from a toddler; a man that she had once called her son. Millie slid back into the passenger seat and put her seat belt on.

"How did it go?" Nicole asked as she pulled away from the curb.

"Smooth," was Millie's response. Now that she was back home, it was her responsibility to get the family back in order. "Everything is so messed up that it may take a little while to get things back on track."

"Where we headed now?" Nicole asked.

"I have to go see a friend that owes me a little something," Millie said with an evil smirk on her face.

Twenty minutes later Nicole pulled up in front of a project building in Harlem and killed the engine. Millie and Nicole entered the building and took the stairs to the third floor. Once Millie found the door, she was looking for she gave it a light knock. Seconds later the sound of feet shuffling from behind the door could be heard followed by several locks being unlocked. The door swung open and a big man with a baldhead and a thick bushy beard stood with a stone look on his face.

"Take that mean look off your face before I do it for you," Millie said. Instantly the big man's face lit up like a Christmas tree.

"Millie!" The big man squealed as he hugged Millie, lifting her off her feet and spinning her around in the process.

"Okay, Knuckles put me down before you kill me by accident," Millie smiled.

Knuckles stepped to the side so Millie and Nicole could enter his apartment. Nicole stepped in the apartment and turned her nose up. The place was filthy and had a scent that she couldn't describe.

"When you get out?" Knuckles asked smiling from ear to ear.

"Just now and you're the first person I came to see," Millie moved a pile of junk from off the couch and sat down. "What have you been doing with yourself?"

"Nothing," Knuckles shrugged his shoulders. He wasn't the sharpest knife in the drawer but he was loyal and a hard worker. "After they took you away, Derrick told me I couldn't work for the family anymore," Knuckles paused for a second. "I almost did something bad to Derrick but I didn't do it because I didn't want you to be mad at me."

"Why would you want to do something bad to Derrick?"

Knuckles looked down at the floor. "Because he called me a retard," he said in a voice barely above a whisper. Millie walked over to Knuckles and hugged him. "You're not a retard. I tell you all the time God made you different because you're special." Millie knew Knuckles was mentally challenged but she could use him in her master plan. "You ready to get back to work?"

"I'm allowed to be back in the family business?" Knuckles said with an excited expression on his face.

"Knuckles, you will always be my family, never forget that. Now get dressed. We got some business to take care of," Millie told him.

Eric Mason

Two

Eric sat in his office with his feet kicked up on his desk watching an episode of a web series he got hooked on called *The Hand I Was Dealt.* Just as the series was getting good, Eric heard a light knock at the door. "Come in!"

Pistol Pete entered the office with a confused look on his face. "Where's Millie? I thought she was supposed to be getting out today?"

"She's out but nobody has heard anything from her yet," Eric leaned back in his leather chair. "I'm sure we'll hear from her sooner or later but be on point. Alex Russo and a few of those Italian fucks supposed to be on their way up here."

"What they want now?"

"They want they hotel back," Eric answered. He knew that the Russo family wouldn't rest until they got their hotel back.

"So, what's the plan?" Pistol Pete asked.

"They can kiss my ass!" Eric snapped. "I paid for this hotel. Now its mines, end of story." As soon as the words left

Eric's lips, his secretary called him and told him that a Mr. Russo was here to see him.

"Send him in."

Alex Russo entered the office along with his son, Frankie, and four strong faced goons.

"Good afternoon, gentlemen. What can I help you with today?" Eric asked in a cool tone.

"I'm here to see if we can work something out," Alex Russo began. "I think we had a misunderstanding. You purchased one of my hotels but it wasn't for sale and I'm here because I want it back." He paused for a second to take in his surroundings. "I'll pay double what you paid for it just so we don't have no hard feelings."

"I wish I could help you," Eric said. "But unfortunately there's nothing I can do for you."

"I don't think you understand," Alex said with a friendly smile. "I'm going to get my hotel back one way or another. For your sake, I'm begging you to consider my offer."

"I'm sorry, are you threatening me?" Eric stood to his feet and immediately one of his bodyguards locked the door.

"Why, yes, I certainly am," Alex said with a straight face. "What you did was wrong and I will not allow you to get away with it. I've been doing business in this city for over forty years and I will not allow some hoodlums like you to come and mess things up."

Pistol Pete quickly reached under the desk, removed an AR-15 assault rifle, and aimed it at the men. Eric slowly walked around his desk and slapped the shit out of Alex Russo. "Don't you ever come into my office and talk to me like that!" Eric growled. "I already told you this hotel is mine. I brought it fair and square. If you have a problem with that then I suggest you take it up with Mr. Chambers because he's the one who signed the contract. Now if you gentlemen would excuse me, I have to get back to work."

Alex Russo rubbed the side of his face and smiled. "I see some people insist on doing things the hard way. I'll be in touch," he said as him and his crew turned and exited the office. Once Alex and his crew left Pistol Pete spoke freely, "I don't know if you should put your hands on that old man."

Eric waved Pistol Pete off. "Fuck him; I ain't sitting here all day listening to bullshit. I have better things to do."

"I understand," Pistol Pete said respectfully. "But right now we don't need any more unnecessary problems. We already have to keep an eye out for the Black Dragon," he reminded him. Eric still had no idea why the assassin known as the Black Dragon wanted him dead. The assassin claimed

6

that someone had given his whereabouts to Chico in return for a reward.

"Fuck Alex and the Black Dragon. I can't sit around all day thinking about those clowns," Eric huffed. In all reality, he was definitely concerned about the Black Dragon. From time to time, Eric found himself peeking over his shoulder trying to catch the danger before it caught him.

"I hear what you saying but we really don't need any more enemies," Pistol Pete told him. "I didn't like the look in Alex's eyes when he left out of here. I say you should have Jimmy take care of that situation before it becomes a real issue."

"I'll call Jimmy in a second," Eric said as he grabbed his things and exited his office. He had an important meeting that he couldn't be late to.

Millie Mason

Three

The white Benz came to a stop in front of a luxury building in downtown Manhattan. Millie, Nicole, and Knuckles stepped out the Benz and made their way to the front of the building. Immediately they were met by the doorman.

"And who are you here to see?" the doorman asked politely.

Millie ignored the doorman and walked past him as if he was invisible, continuing on towards the elevator.

"Millie, I think that guy was talking to us," Knuckles pointed out.

"We don't talk to strangers." Millie patted Knuckles cheek gently as the trio boarded the elevator. The elevator reached the eighteenth floor before the doors dinged open. Millie strolled down the hallway until she found the door she was looking for and rang the doorbell. Seconds later a Spanish man in an expensive looking suit answered the door with a smile on his face. "Millie, Millie, Millie," he sang showing every last one of his teeth. "What a pleasant surprise." He stepped to the side so the trio could enter.

"Cut the shit, Julio. You know why I'm here," Millie huffed. "Before I went to prison you were paying 15% for protection fees. As soon as I went to jail your payments suddenly stopped and now I hear that for the past year you've had your men in territory that belongs to the Mason family."

"Let's have a drink," Julio walked over to his bar area and poured everyone a drink. Millie stepped further into the luxury apartment and spotted several half-naked women sitting around. Julio returned and handed Millie a glass. Millie disrespectfully slapped the glass out of Julio's hand.

"I'm here to talk business!" Millie snapped. "I'm going to need you to start paying for protection again. And instead of 15% now I'm going to have to charge you 30% since you have your men on territory that belongs to me."

Julio chuckled. "Listen Millie, this ain't back in the day no more. You've been gone a long time and a lot of things have changed." Julio wasn't about to let Millie walk up in his spot and change how he'd been doing things, especially since she had been gone for almost twenty years. "Millie, you know I got nothing but love for you. I heard about the hardship that you and your family has been going through so if you ever get a little strapped for cash you can always come and work for me," Julio said with an evil smirk on his face.

That last comment got a few giggles out of some of the ladies that sat around.

Millie took a step closer toward Julio. "I didn't come here to fuck around and since you want to be a smart ass the price just went up to 40%,"

"Stop fucking playing with me, bitch!" Julio barked. "You ain't getting shit from me so you can take your taxes and shove them up your pretty little ass!"

"That's not how you should speak to a lady," Knuckles stepped in.

Julio looked at Knuckles and busted out in a dramatic laugh. "Listen, you retard. I talk how I want in my shit!"

As soon as Knuckles heard the word "retard" leave Julio's lips, he snapped. "I'm not retarded!" he roared as he grabbed Julio by his shirt and tossed him across the room as if he were a baby. Julio crashed violently into the wall unit. Before Julio got a chance to recover, Knuckles was already on top of him rearranging his face with each punch landed. Millie looked on with a smile on her face. She kept Knuckles around for a reason. He was a good person but if you got on his bad side, it was hell to pay. Knuckles stomped Julio out then reached down and lifted Julio up over his head. Without warning, Knuckles ran and tossed Julio out the eighteenth floor window. Just as the ladies in the house were about to scream, Nicole pulled out her silenced .380 and put all five of the half-naked women down before they could even process what was going on. Millie walked over and rubbed Knuckles back gently. "Calm down, it's going to be alright."

"I'm not retarded," Knuckles whined as his chest heaved up and down. He knew he was different but there was something about being called out that drove him over the edge.

"Listen Knuckles, I'm home now. You don't ever have to worry about anything ever again," Millie promised. She didn't know how Knuckles had made it this long with her being away for such a long time. Ever since they were kids, Millie had always looked after Knuckles and treated him like a normal person when everyone teased and made fun of him. "Come on; let's go get something to eat."

The Black Dragon
Four

The Black Dragon stepped off the Greyhound bus with a no-nonsense look on his face. He rode on the bus for hours to get to New York just because they weren't allowed to search his bags on the bus. The Black Dragon grabbed his bag and made his way towards the subway. Inside his bag were all of his favorite killing instruments. He stood up on the train and thought about how he was going to kill Eric for double-crossing him. The Black Dragon stepped off the train and headed straight for the hole in the wall motel he would be staying at during this trip. Once inside the room, the Black Dragon dumped all his weapons out on the bed, changed into all black, and grabbed his weapons of choice. Then he headed right back out the door. He had business to take care of.

The Black Dragon pulled up across the street from the hotel that Eric owned and placed the gear in park. The Black Dragon grabbed his .380 from off the passenger seat, attached the silencer to the barrel, then stepped out the car and made his way across the street. The Black Dragon stepped in the hotel and headed straight for the front desk.

"May I help you?" the blonde hair receptionist asked with a big friendly smile on her face.

"Yes, I'm looking for Eric Mason," he said.

"I'm sorry but he's not here today," she replied.

"Well, it's really important that I speak with him. Is there any way you can call him for me?" the Black Dragon asked as he gave a friendly smile.

"I'm sorry, sir. I have no way to get in touch with him," the receptionist said. "But I'm sure he'll definitely be in tomorrow if you wanted to come back and try again."

The Black Dragon smiled. "No, that won't be necessary. I'm sure I'll track him down before the night is out. You have a good night," he said politely as he turned and made his exit.

As soon as the Black Dragon exited the hotel, the receptionist quickly walked to the back room, went down a flight of stairs, then turned down a narrow hallway, and knocked on the door.

Pistol Pete answered the door. "Hey, Brittany. What's up?"

"Sorry, don't mean to bother you guys. Just thought y'all should know that a scary looking man dressed in all black just came by looking for Eric."

Eric sat behind a desk along with two other men counting a table full of cash. "Was he dark skin with a low hair cut?" Eric asked.

Brittany nodded. "Yup."

"Low eyes and a thin mustache?"

"Yup, that's him," Brittany confirmed.

Eric walked over to Brittany and handed her a hundred dollar bill. "Keep up the good work," he said.

"Thank you," Brittany said then made her exit. Once she was out of the room Eric spoke freely. "I knew the Black Dragon would be coming for me sooner or later. Tell everyone to strap up and be on point."

"More than likely he'll be outside scoping the building waiting on you to come and go," Pistol Pete said.

"Good. Round up a couple of shooters and go air his car out," Eric ordered.

"I'm on it," Pistol Pete said as he left to go handle his business.

Jimmy Mason
Five

Jimmy sat in the passenger seat of the silver Range Rover sipping on a cup of Effen vodka. It was a nasty rainy night and, as usual, Jimmy was up to no good. "Yo, slow down before you get us pulled over."

Murder sat behind the wheel bobbing his head to the sound of Remy Ma's new mixtape. "Yo, where we headed?"

"Eric just called me and told me he needs us to go rough up some fake Italian dudes," Jimmy shrugged. Jimmy had no clue who the Russo family was nor did he care. If Eric wanted them taken care of, it was as good as done.

"What Italian dudes?"

"Frank and Alex Russo," Jimmy answered.

"I heard of those clowns," Murder said. "I think they got connects with the mob. You sure that's who Eric wants us to hit?"

"You sound scared." Jimmy took a sip from his cup. "This ain't the 80's no more. Fuck the mob."

Murder laughed. "You a funny guy. I was just asking because of all of the heat that's been coming down on the family." Murder pulled up in front of a low-key bar and killed the engine.

"Yo, pop the trunk!" Jimmy said as he smoothly stepped out the passenger seat, made his way to the trunk, and removed a wooden baseball bat. Jimmy stepped inside the bar and immediately all eyes were on him and Murder. Jimmy walked up to the closest person to him and swung the baseball bat with all his might. The entire bar watched in horror as Jimmy beat the innocent man to a bloody pulp with the baseball bat. Once Jimmy was done, he walked over to the bar and helped himself to a seat. "Vodka and orange juice!" The bartender quickly made Jimmy's drink and sat it down in front of him. Jimmy downed the drink in a few gulps then stood back to his feet. "I'm looking for Frank or Alex Russo. Anyone know where I can find either one of them?" Everyone remained quiet.

Murder walked up and shot three men who sat at the bar in the head.

BLOCKA!

BLOCKA!

BLOCKA!

"Now I'm going to ask y'all one more time!" Jimmy barked. "Do anyone know where I can find Frank or Alex Russo?"

"They just left about twenty minutes ago!" the bartender spoke up.

Jimmy slowly walked over towards the bartender. "Do you mind delivering a message for me?"

"Of course I don't mind," he said.

"Tell them to stay the fuck out of the Mason's family business before this shit get real ugly. You think you can do that for me?" Jimmy asked with a smirk on his face.

"Yes sir," the bartender replied with a terrified look on his face.

Jimmy reached over the counter and grabbed a bottle of vodka. "Thank you," he said as him and Murder made their exit.

＝

Eric Mason

Six

Eric sat in his living room talking to Pistol Pete. The two were trying to come up with a strategy on how they were going to handle this Black Dragon situation. "I say we hit him before he gets us," Pistol Pete suggested.

"I say we should maybe set him up and lead him into a trap," Eric said. He figured that would be better than just going to war with a professional assassin. "We know he'll be following us so I say we have a bunch of our soldiers waiting at one of our warehouses or something and lead the Black Dragon into a deadly trap."

Pistol Pete rubbed his chin. "That doesn't sound like a bad idea. Now all we have to do is find the perfect spot."

Before Eric could say another word, he saw Millie, Nicole, and some big strong looking guy being escorted through his mansion.

"The Queen is back," Millie smiled as she leaned in and gave Eric a tight hug followed by a kiss on the cheek.

"We thought you had got lost for a second," Eric laughed. He couldn't hide the excitement on his face. At heart, he would always be a momma's boy. "I'm glad you're here. Pistol Pete and I were just trying to come up with a little plan. A lot of stuff has been going on while you were away," Eric said happy to have his mother back in his corner.

"Before we get started, I want to introduce you guys to someone," Millie said. "This here is Knuckles. He's family."

"I remember you when you was this little," Knuckles said holding his hands not far apart from one another as he looked at Eric with a bright smile on his face.

"Well, welcome to the family and I look forward to working with you," Eric said as him and Knuckles shook hands. He then turned his focus back on Millie. "We have a bit of a problem."

Millie helped herself to a seat on the couch and crossed her legs. "Hit me with it."

"I'll go get everyone a drink," Nicole got up and excused herself so that they could talk business.

"Remember that assassin I hired to take out Chico's family?"

Millie nodded.

"Well, someone told him that I gave his whereabouts to Chico and now he wants me dead," Eric explained. "I have no clue why he would think that I gave him up to Chico."

Millie sat on the couch with a straight face. There was no way she was going to tell Eric that it was her who had told Chico about the Black Dragon's whereabouts. "Listen son, if the Black Dragon wants to go to war then I say we take him to war."

"We also have a problem with the Russo family," Eric said. "I bought one of their hotels and now they want their hotel back and it doesn't look like they're willing to take no for an answer."

Millie sucked her teeth. "The Russo family still out here making noise?" She remembered having a run in with the Russo family back in the day. "Listen, I'll go and talk to Frank Russo. Me and him have a little history." Millie stood to her feet. "But I have to get going. I have a few things that needs my immediate attention. I'll call you later," Millie said as she and Knuckles made their exit.

Eric got ready to finish his conversation with Pistol Pete when he heard Nicole clear her throat. "Hey baby, can I have a word with you in the room for a second?"

"Of course," Eric stood to his feet and headed to their bedroom. "Hey, baby. What's up?"

"Is everything alright? I overheard a little bit of the conversation back there," Nicole said with a nervous look on her face. "Why didn't you tell me that your life or that our life was in danger?"

"Sorry, baby. I didn't want to worry you," he replied.

"Eric, we are supposed to be a team. You can't have me walking out here blindly." Nicole put on her mad face. The truth was, Nicole had already known about the Black Dragon hit. She just wanted something to fuss about. "What if something would have happened to me while I was out? Then what?"

Eric positioned himself behind Nicole and gently began to rub her shoulders. "You are absolutely right baby and I'm sorry. Some assassin that goes by the name the Black Dragon is out to kill me."

"Why?"

"Because he thinks that I gave his whereabouts to an enemy of his." Eric paused for a second. "I have no idea where he could have gotten a thought like that from."

"Well, just know that I got your back and as long as I'm around I won't let anyone hurt you," Nicole smiled.

"Get over here!" Eric playfully tossed Nicole on the bed and straddled her. "You still love me?"

"No matter what."

Frank Russo

Seven

Frank Russo sat in his office with a cold look on his face and a strong drink in his hand. He had just gotten word about what Jimmy Mason had done to one of his bars. The more he thought about the Mason family the angrier he became. Sitting in front of him were two of his best enforcers. First was a big man that went by the name Lethal Weapon. He got that name because he was a killing machine and known to turn any object he touches into a lethal weapon. Sitting next to him was a man with a mean scowl on his face. A man that went by the name Bad News. Bad News was well known by the law for his violent ways. Back in the day, it was said that he was a hitman for the mob and had a lot of bodies under his belt.

"I have a problem," Frank Russo began. "And their name is the Mason family. They've been nothing but a pain in the ass since the first time I had a run in with them back in the 90's. I need you two to get rid of the Mason family for me once and for all," Frank barked. He was getting old in age and refused to let the Mason Family bully him around and take over the all the businesses that he had worked so hard to maintain.

"This is going to be a piece of cake," Lethal Weapon waved him off. "I thought you had a real problem," he said arrogantly.

"The Mason family ain't no joke so please be careful," Frank warned.

Lethal Weapon chuckled. "I ain't no joke either."

Later On That Night

Lethal Weapon pulled up in front of Eric's hotel and killed the engine. On the passenger seat sat an AR-15 assault rifle. "Time to go to work," Lethal Weapon said to himself as he rolled a ski mask down over his face, grabbed the rifle from off the front seat, and headed inside the hotel. Lethal Weapon strolled into the lobby of the hotel and opened fire on any and everything moving. He waved his arms from side to side, as the assault rifle rattled in his hands dropping innocent civilians like flies. Once his clip was empty, Lethal Weapon back peddled out of the hotel and sprinted back to his car.

Eight

D errick sat in the mess hall eating lunch when a guy that went by the name Russel sat down next to him.

"Yo, you ain't hear this from me but I heard a couple of Italian dudes are supposed to be running down on you today," Russel whispered.

"Word?" Derrick asked while still eating his food. He didn't know what was going on but he was thankful for Russel giving him the heads up.

"Yeah, I heard the Mason family and the Russo family going hard at each other out there in them streets," Russel said.

Derrick nodded his head as if this wasn't news to him but the truth was he had no clue what was going on out on the streets. Ever since Millie had been home, he hadn't heard a word from her or anyone else in the family for that matter. "Good looking."

"No doubt," Russel said as he knocked on the table, stood up, and then made his exit. Derrick finished his meal and stood up. As he went to dump his tray, someone hit him hard tackling him down to the floor from behind. Derrick hit the floor and spun around just in time to see an Italian man coming towards him holding a shank in his hand. With one Italian man's arms wrapped around his waist and another one moving in on him, it forced his survival skills to kick in. Derrick quickly took his fingers and clawed the eyes of the Italian man that had tackled him and held him around the waist. The Italian man howled in pain before releasing his grip on Derrick. Derrick quickly shot to his feet and grabbed a hold of the wrist of the knifed man. The Italian man landed a vicious head butt that caused all the inmates that were now standing on their feet in mess hall to roar. Some men rooting for the Italian men while the others rooted and cheered for Derrick.

The two men struggled and fought over the shank, neither one wanting to be on the receiving end of the sharp blade. Once the Italian man realized that he wouldn't be able to get Derrick to release the grip that he held on his wrist he quickly resorted to Plan B. Without warning the Italian man dropped the shank, dipped low, and scooped Derrick's legs up from under him causing both men to hit the floor hard. Derrick landed on the bottom but held a firm grip around the Italian man's head and neck. Derrick applied pressure to the chokehold. As soon as it seemed like the Italian man was about to pass out several correctional officers came and broke up the fight separating the two men.

Nine

Bad News pulled up in front of a lounge that was located in the middle of the hood. He had gotten word that Jimmy Mason would be at this lounge tonight celebrating his comrade's birthday. Bad News decided to crash the party. He couldn't think of a better way to make an example out of Jimmy than to kill him in front of all of the losers that looked up to him. Bad News stepped out of his vehicle and made his way towards the entrance of the lounge. Immediately, he spotted several men loitering in front of the entrance smoking weed and loud talking.

"Look at this motherfucker," one of the men said loudly causing the rest of his buddies to laugh. "This fool must be lost. Hey, dickhead! You know where the fuck you at?"

Bad News ignored the men who stood out front. He had hoped and prayed that one of them would have tried to make a move on him but luckily for them they hadn't. He entered the lounge and headed straight for the bar where he ordered a drink, then stood off to the side and took in his surroundings. Bad News watched as women danced on women. He thought it was strange how all the men seemed to be too cool to dance. Instead, they all stood around with drinks in their hands and mean looks on their faces. Bad News walked around the lounge sipping his drink when he spotted Jimmy Mason and some big booty girl over in the cut arguing. Bad News had no clue who the girl was but from the looks of it, she was furious with Jimmy and she wasn't afraid to let him know. Bad News stood off to the side and continued to watch Jimmy. He made sure he watched him closely as he tried to pinpoint how many of the men that stood around Jimmy were his main muscle. Bad News watched as one of Jimmy's main goons headed to the bathroom. He smoothly slid off the wall and followed the rough faced looking man into the men's room. Bad News figured he'd start with taking out the muscle first. He squeezed his way through the crowd and pushed his way inside the men's room. Immediately, Bad News noticed that the rest room was empty except for Jimmy's rough faced friend. He quickly removed a sharp wire from the sleeves of his trench coat. Bad News faked like he was about to use the urinal beside the rough faced man and as soon as he saw an opening he looped the wire around the man's neck and applied a tremendous amount of pressure. The rough faced man peed all over his shoes as he fought and struggled to try and remove the wire from around his neck but it was no use. The more he tried to remove the wire from around his neck, the more the wire cut through his skin cutting off his circulation and his access to oxygen. Bad News kept applying pressure to the wire until finally the man stopped moving and his body laid limp on the dirty bathroom floor. Once that was done, he quickly exited the rest room. His next target was Jimmy Mason.

Ten

"**B**ut why you gotta be all up in that girl's face?" Cherokee huffed, all up in Jimmy's face. "You want me to go over there and slap the bitch or something?"

"Chill out, baby. I was just talking to her," Jimmy said trying to downplay what his intentions really were.

"Talking to her about what?" Cherokee folded her arms across her chest.

"I know shorty from high school. What's the big deal?" Jimmy said, now with an attitude. "Listen if you going to be acting all insecure anytime some beautiful ladies come around then I'm going to have to demote you," he said in a slick tone.

"Demote me?" Cherokee echoed. Before Jimmy could fix his mouth to say another word, Cherokee had already swung on him. "Don't you ever try to play me like I'm some chick that you just met!" she yelled as she managed to punch Jimmy in his face three times and rip his shirt before security got a chance to get her up off of him. "You better not come home tonight motherfucker!" she yelled as security escorted her towards the exit.

"You cancelled!" Jimmy yelled over the loud music with an embarrassed look on his face.

"You good?" Murder asked coming over to Jimmy's side with a concerned look on his face.

"Yeah, I'm good," Jimmy said trying to fix his shirt but it was no use. Cherokee had ripped it at the collar. Having no other choice, Jimmy removed his shirt and just rocked a plain white wife beater.

"As soon as I seen shorty with that big ole ass talking to you I already knew it was about to be problems," Murder laughed.

Jimmy's laugh quickly came to an end when he saw a big Italian man knock two of his henchmen out cold with one punch.

***

Bad News reached Jimmy's VIP section and knocked out two men he saw leaning up against the rail trying to look cool. He was tired of sitting back waiting. He knew he was out numbered but Bad News loved a challenge. Bad News grabbed another one of Jimmy's goons and violently snapped his neck. He went to move on to the next man when a champagne bottle shattered violently over his head from behind. One of Jimmy's goons, a big man named Beans, who had just came home from jail after doing seven years, grabbed Bad News from behind. The two big men tussled until finally Beans and Bad News flipped over the rail and went crashing violently down to the slippery floor. Once Jimmy realized what was going on he quickly hopped over the rail as him and the rest of his team proceeded to stomp the big man out.

"Is you crazy! Come up in my party acting stupid!" Jimmy growled as he violently stomped the big man's head down into the floor. Somehow, Bad News managed to climb up from off the floor. His face was a bloody mess but still he held a sickening smile on his face. Bad News dropped two more of Jimmy's goons with wild haymakers as he began to backpedal towards the exit. Murder weaved one of the big man's punches and stabbed him in the rib area with his pocketknife. "Don't try to run now, motherfucker!" Murder yelled as he stabbed the big man several times before several bouncers came to Bad News's rescue. The bouncers quickly stopped Jimmy's crew from killing the Italian man.

"Chill, there's too many witnesses in here!" one of the bouncers yelled at Jimmy snapping him out of his trance. For a second Jimmy had blacked out and all he saw was red.

"Get that white boy the fuck up out of here before I kill him!" Jimmy warned. The bouncer was right. The place was packed with eyewitnesses and the last thing Jimmy needed was another charge. "Yo!" Jimmy called Murder over. Jimmy removed his 9mm from the small of his back, reached down in his pocket, screwed the silencer onto the barrel, and discreetly handed the gun to Murder. "Go outside and take care of that clown."

Murder nodded and turned heading for the exit. Murder stepped outside and looked up and down the street. "Damn!" Murder cursed. The Italian man was nowhere in sight.

Eric Mason

Eleven

Eric stepped out his front door and slid in the back seat of the Range Rover. He had just gotten several calls from employees at his hotel informing him that someone had walked in the lobby and shot the place up along with several members of his staff. "The Black Dragon?" Eric asked.

"Nope," Pistol Pete answered making sure to keep his eyes on the road. "From what I'm hearing it was an Italian man."

"Frank Russo must of sent one of his men to shoot up the hotel cause I wouldn't sell it back to him," Eric shook his head. He knew the Russo family wasn't going to go away quietly. Now he had to find a way to end this feud before things really got out of hand.

"What's the play boss?" Pistol Pete asked as he pulled up in front of the hotel.

"I'm not sure yet," Eric replied. He slipped out the back seat and entered his hotel to see just how much damage had been done. He stepped inside his place of business when he was confronted by a serious-faced detective.

"Detective, Tyson," he flashed his badge. "Mind if I ask you a few questions?"

"Sure, be my guest," Eric replied.

"Let me start off by saying I did my research on your family before I got here and I was disgusted," Detective Tyson began. "I know all about you and from what I hear you're a real scum bag,"

"I don't mean to cut you off detective but are we almost done here? I have a very important meeting that I have to get to," Eric said with a friendly smile on his face. He hated cops and everything they stood for.

"I got my eye on you. One slip and that's your ass!" Detective Tyson growled as he brushed past Eric he made sure that he forcefully bumped shoulders with him on his way out.

"Have a nice day!" Eric called over his shoulder. He then looked over to Pistol Pete. "Get me all the info you can on that detective," Eric ordered. He wanted to know everything there was to know about the detective that way he'd know what he was up against. Eric looked up and almost shit in his pants. Getting off the elevator up ahead was none other than the Black Dragon. His presence alone was enough to send chills up Eric's spine. The Black Dragon was the last person he expected to see on a day like this. Eric reached in his suit jack and gripped the handle of his P89 when he felt a pair of hands touch him from behind causing him to almost jump out of his skin. Eric spun around with a crazy look in his eyes ready to squeeze the trigger but he let up when he saw who stood in front of him.

"What's wrong baby? You look like you just saw a ghost. Is everything alright?" Nicole asked.

"He...hey baby, what you doing here?" Eric asked stumbling over his words.

"I came to take my man out to lunch. I know you've been having a rough week so I figured I'd come and take your mind off of work for a little while."

"Now is not a good time, baby," Eric said as he grabbed Nicole's arm and pushed her towards the staircase.

"Eric, you're hurting me!" Nicole snatched her arm out of his grip. "What the hell is wrong with you?"

Eric pulled his P89 from his holster with a nervous look on his face. "Come on, baby, we have to go. The assassin is here! And he's coming to kill me!" Eric rushed Nicole down the flight of stairs. They made it down two flights when they heard the staircase door bust open followed by the sound of feet running down the stairs skipping two at a time. "Come on, come on, come on!" Eric yelled in a panicked tone as he and Nicole went spilling out the side door that led out into the garage area. Nicole ran and slipped her hand down in her purse and removed her .380. Without warning, she quickly turned and tackled Eric, forcing him down behind a parked car just as two bullets whizzed past her head. "Stay down!" Nicole whispered as she darted from behind the parked car and fired off three shots in the Black Dragon's direction, before diving behind another parked car. Eric looked on with a shocked look on his face. Seeing Nicole move like this was all new to him. And just from first glance, he could tell that this wasn't her first rodeo.

Nicole stayed low as she listened for the Black Dragon's movements. She reached down in her purse and tossed a smoke bomb over her shoulder. The smoke bomb exploded and immediately filled the garage up with a thick cloudy smoke.

***

The Black Dragon stood behind a wall as he watched the smoke bomb land and immediately fill the garage with smoke. He had no clue who this mystery woman was but whoever she was he had to admit she had skills. The Black Dragon sprung from behind the wall and eased his way through the parking garage with a firm two-handed grip on his gun. Not being able to see, the Black Dragon had to use his ears as his eyes. He inched his way through the garage when he heard the sound of tires screeching. The Black Dragon turned his head just in the nick of time to see a pair of headlights coming straight at him. "Shit!" the Black Dragon yelled as he jumped out of the way just as the car zoomed past him. He hit the floor, rolled, and came up firing but it was no use. The car had already sped out of the parking garage.

Nicole

Twelve

Nicole weaved from lane to lane at a high speed her eyes going from the road to the rear view mirror then back to the road.

"What the hell was that back there?" Eric asked staring at Nicole. He had just seen a new side to her; a dangerous, violent side.

"What?" Nicole asked faking ignorance. "I got us up out of there."

"You've been playing me all this time!" Eric barked as he banged his fist on the dashboard.

Nicole quickly pulled over to the side of the road and placed the gear in park. "Playing you how? I just saved our lives," she shot back.

"How'd you learn how to shoot like that?" Eric pressed. "Those were professional skills you showed back there!"

"I didn't want to say anything, but I used to be an assassin in my past life," Nicole admitted only telling half of the truth.

"Why weren't you honest with me from the beginning?"

"Didn't want to scare you off," Nicole answered. "Ain't no man going to want to make no female assassin his wife," she pointed out.

"When we get back to the house I want you to pack your things and get the fuck out of my house!" Eric spat. He loved Nicole to death but he couldn't trust her any longer. The fact that she was able to keep a secret for that long bothered him.

"Baby, you're overreacting," Nicole pleaded. "I love you. Please don't do this to us."

"You did this to yourself," Eric said with ice in his tone. He was so mad that he didn't even want to look at Nicole.

Nicole placed the gear back in drive and pulled back out into traffic. "I'm sorry," she said in a light whispered. "I wanted to tell you but your mother told me not to."

Eric turned and looked at Nicole. "I don't want to hear another word from you, do I make myself clear?"

"Crystal clear!" Nicole said matching Eric's tone.

When they arrived back at the mansion, Nicole stormed inside and headed straight for the master bedroom. Eric walked over to the bar and poured himself a strong drink as he heard the sound of glass shatter coming from upstairs. He figured she was probably upstairs breaking all of his things. Eric sipped his drink as he slowly made his way upstairs. He stepped in the bedroom and saw Nicole standing with a golf club in her hand. She tried to break anything that wasn't glued down to the floor.

"What the hell are you doing?" Eric asked with his face crumbled up.

"What does it look like I'm doing? I'm tearing shit up!" Nicole yelled as she swung the gulf club and shattered the mirror that sat on top of the dresser. "I hope you and you're new bitch have a good time cleaning all this shit up!" She went to swing the gulf club again but Eric grabbed her from behind in a bear hug.

"Stop with all this bullshit. Just get your shit and get the fuck out!" Eric growled.

Nicole dipped low and hip tossed Eric down to the floor. Before Eric knew what was going on, he looked up, and was staring down the barrel of a 9mm. Nicole stood over Eric with her gun pointed at his head.

"Baby, put the gun down," Eric said in a soft tone. He didn't want to come off aggressive and wind up getting his head blown off so he decided to play it cool. "Baby, listen. Trust me; you don't want to do this."

"Oh, now I'm your baby," Nicole sang sarcastically. "Was I your baby a few seconds ago when you told me to get my shit and get the fuck out? Huh?"

"Listen, baby. I'm going to need you to put that gun down," Eric slowly raised his hands in surrender.

"You know you're the only family I got," Nicole said as tears rolled down her face. "And this is how you do me?" she said as she lowered the gun and tossed it on the bed. "You don't have to worry about me ever again." Nicole turned and made her exit, leaving Eric lying in the middle of the floor with a stressed out look on his face.

Beans
Thirteen

Beans stepped out the building carrying a small duffle bag in his hand. He flipped his hood over his head as he cautiously looked over both shoulders before heading down the block to where his car was parked. Beans had only been out of jail for a few weeks and was already back working for the Mason family. All the time he spent up north in jail did him no good. Prison was supposed to be a rehabilitation center for criminals but all it did was teach and mold Beans into a master criminal; a more violent criminal who would rather hold court in the street before going back to prison. As Beans made his way up the block, he never noticed the four pairs of eyes that were on him the entire time.

***

Lethal Weapon sat behind the wheel of a black Ford Explorer with a pissed off look on his face. "So you mean to tell me this is the guy that fucked you up?"

"I told you already," Bad News huffed. "I got jumped by like six of those moolies and they still couldn't even get me off my feet," he boasted. Bad News winced in pain as he grabbed at one of his stab wounds.

"You see this is why you need me around," Lethal Weapon threw the gear into drive and began to follow Bean's car. "Now I'm going to show you how to kill a man the right way." Lethal Weapon loved Bad News like a brother and the fact that someone had actually physically assaulted him didn't sit well with him. From the time he heard the news, Lethal Weapon knew that he was going to hunt down each man one by one and make him pay for what they had done to his partner. "You can sit this one out tonight. I got it," Lethal Weapon said keeping his eyes on the road.

"Not happening," Bad News protested quickly. "I'm going to make that motherfucker pay for what him and his friends did to me."

***

Beans stepped in his home and was instantly bum rushed by his two sons.

"Wassup, dad! You up for a game of Madden?" Jacob, the older of the two boys, asked.

"Damn, can I even get in the door first?" Beans joked as he turned to his other son, an eight year old that went by the name Travis. "And what you want?"

"I want to show you this new back flip I just learned how to do," Travis said with an excited smile on his face.

"Thank god you're home," Iyana the mother of his two children said as she leaned in and kissed Beans on the lips.

"Thank god I'm home, my ass," Beans joked. "Why don't I smell nothing cooking?" He looked down at his watch then back up to Iyanna. "What you on strike or something?"

"The kids wanted to do pizza tonight so I told them that they had to wait until you got home because I wasn't sure what you would be in the mood for it when you got here."

Beans took a step closer and palmed Iyana's ass with one hand until one of the kids finally cleared his throat, reminding them that they were still standing right there. "My bad," Beans laughed. On the streets, Beans was one of the roughest men to walk the streets and feared by many men but at home, he was the sweetest and most gentle person you could ever meet. It was like night and day with him. Out on the streets Beans was a beast but when in the house he was a family man. Beans and his family sat around watching an episode of *Martin* when he heard a loud knock at the door. "Oh, that must be the pizza." Beans stood up and headed to the door. He opened the door without looking through the peephole and was rewarded with a broken nose. Lethal Weapon violently smashed the butt of the assault rifle in his face. "Everybody down on the floor!" Lethal Weapon yelled as he sent several rounds into the ceiling. He roughly snatched Beans up off the floor by the collar of his shirt and forced him inside the living room with the rest of the family.

Bad News entered the house last and closed the door behind him. He walked into the living room and smiled when he saw Beans with a scared look on his face and blood leaking from his nose. Bad News pulled a roll of duct tape from his back pocket and quickly taped Beans' entire family's mouth and hands.

"You done fucked with the wrong motherfuckers," Lethal Weapon said with an evil smirk on his face. He reached down in his back pocket and removed a hammer. Lethal Weapon walked over towards the youngest son and without warning, he raised the hammer and struck the child in the face. Iyana and Beans let out muffled screams from behind the tape that covered their mouths as they watched in horror as Lethal Weapon repeatedly hit the young child in the face and head with the hammer until he was no longer moving. Lethal Weapon then moved on to the next child. Beans shut his eyes as he heard the hammer striking his other son. The scene was too much for him to take in.

"Are we having fun yet?" Lethal Weapon asked, his face covered in specs of blood as he now stood in front of Iyana. Lethal Weapon ignored her muffled cries and swung the hammer with all his might repeatedly until Iyana stopped moving. Lethal Weapon moved on to Beans but stopped short when he heard Bad News speak for the first time.

"Nah, I want him!" Bad News stepped up. He removed a sharp hunting knife from the small of his back.

"Hold on, I think he's trying to say something," Lethal Weapon said as he roughly snatched the strip of tape from Beans mouth.

"When Jimmy finds out what happened to me and my family he's going to hunt the both of you down!" Beans growled.

Bad News jammed the knife in and out of Beans chest repeatedly until his arm got tired. Lethal Weapon quickly searched the house for a stash before the duo made their exit.

Millie Mason
Fourteen

Millie sat in the passenger seat of the forest green Range Rover staring out the window. In her hand was a white Styrofoam cup filled with vodka and a sprinkle of orange juice. "And then what happened?"

"Then he told me to get the fuck out." Nicole wiped her eyes dry. For the last twenty minutes, she had been telling Millie about the big fight that she had with Eric.

"All the time that I've known you, you know I've never seen you cry," Millie pointed out.

"But what was I supposed to do? Let him get killed?"

"You did the right thing," Millie said in a soft voice. "I'll talk to my son and fix this but right now I need you focused." Tonight Millie had an important meeting with Chico. The Mason family needed some product and at the moment, he was their only option.

Knuckles pulled the Range Rover up in front of the five star hotel and the trio quickly stepped out the SUV as the valet attendant hopped in. Millie led the trio to the restaurant inside the hotel. She walked past the hostess and headed straight for the table in the back.

Chico sat at the table enjoying a nice dinner along with four heavily armed bodyguards. He looked up and saw Millie standing before him. Behind her was a pretty woman that looked to be maybe fifteen or twenty years younger and behind her was a huge man who looked like an NFL linebacker. Immediately, Chico's team of bodyguards frisked the trio before allowing them to have a seat at the table.

"Millie, what do I owe the pleasure?" Chico asked, not bothering to look up from his plate.

"I need some product and I need a lot of it," Millie answered.

"I'm sure that you're aware that I no longer do any business with the Mason family. Your reputation is no good anymore." Chico took a long sip from his glass of wine. "Besides, the Mason family cannot be trusted."

"Oh, but you trusted me when I gave you the Black Dragon's info? Or how about all the millions I made for you before I went to prison," Millie refreshed his memory. "Chico you know me and you know what I'm about."

"A lot of things has changed since you been gone," Chico said. "Your son is responsible for getting my closest loved ones murdered including my daughter so there's no way that I'd ever do business with the Mason family again."

"You put a hit on him and his entire family. What was he supposed to do?"

"The answer is no!" Chico said in a stern tone. He was tired of beating around the bush and making small talk with Millie even though he liked and respected her. She was a hard worker and great businesswoman but there was no way that Chico would be able to forgive the Mason family for all the pain that they had caused.

"Chico, I strongly urge you to reconsider," Millie said, the look on her face serious. "If I walk out of here I go from a potential ally back to the competition and I don't think you want that."

Chico chuckled. "I'll take my chances," he smirked.

Millie nodded as she stood to her feet. "Thanks for your time," she said as she and her team made their exit.

***

Millie slid back into the passenger seat and slammed her hand down on the dashboard. "Could you believe how that asshole spoke to me?"

"I mean, you couldn't actually believe that Chico was going to sit down and do business with you?" Nicole asked.

"I knew he wouldn't agree to do business with me, I just wanted to look him in the eyes," Millie said. "I have a meeting with a new connect. One that can supply us with as much product as we need."

"What's the connect's name?" Nicole asked.

"He goes by the name Brady."

"I've heard stories about him. Heard he's the real deal," Nicole said. "Out in Miami I heard he's more popular than the president."

"I'm going to make Chico regret not selling to the Mason family," Millie smiled. "We going to put that fucker out of business."

"When are we heading to Miami?" Nicole asked from the back seat.

Millie turned and looked back at Nicole with a smile on her face. "Tonight."

Frank Russo

Fifteen

F rank Russo sat in his office listening to Bad News and Lethal Weapon go into detail about all the events that had taken place in the past forty-eight hours. Frank listened with a smile on his face. He was happy to hear that the Mason family was finally starting to take some losses on their end. "Next I want that cocksucker Eric to suffer. No way I'm letting him get away with stealing my hotel," Frank said in a stern tone.

"I went and shot up the hotel like you asked," Lethal Weapon smiled. "What's next?"

"I want you to set Eric's house on fire," Frank said with a wicked look on his face. "And I want you to do it while he's home."

Lethal Weapon smiled. "Now you're speaking my language."

"What about me? What do you need me to do?" Bad News asked not wanting to be left out.

"Your job is to take out Jimmy Mason," Frank Russo said. "I want you to make his life a living hell until those scumbags decides to give me my hotel back."

Bad News nodded his head. "That won't be a problem."

"I want the pressure put on these moolies. Let them know we ain't fucking around!" Frank barked. "I want my hotel back!"

Brady
Sixteen

B rady sat in his back yard enjoying a nice drink while his accountant ran some numbers by him. Brady only half listened due to the distraction. In front of him, in his swimming pool, were ten naked models playing volleyball. The models played volleyball, sniffed coke, and listened to music all at the same time. "Hey, Dave, let's wrap this up. I have some very important guests that should be arriving here any minute." Brady finished off his drink and shook his accountant's hand. "One of my bodyguards will escort you out."

Once his accountant was gone, Brady turned to his best friend and second in charge; a man that went by the name Slim. "I want that motherfucker dead before the night is out," Brady said in a calm tone. "Stealing from me and think I wouldn't find out."

"You want it quick and easy or you want it to be messy?" Slim asked.

"Messy," Brady answered as the maid came over and prepared him another drink. "Now tell me what you know about this Millie chick that's supposed to be meeting with us today?"

"I did a little research on her and her family," Slim began. "Everything checked out she seems to be official. She got popped and did a fifteen year bid and never said a word."

Brady nodded his head. "I like her already."

"Only thing is, she works with her family and I don't know how I feel about that," Slim added. "But besides that she seems to be the real deal."

"We'll hear her out when she gets here," Brady said. His eyes were glued to the volleyball match that was taking place in his pool. Two drinks later one of Brady's bodyguards came and whispered in his ear. "Some lady named Millie is out front. Says she has a meeting with you today."

"Yeah, send her in," Brady ordered. He stood to his feet and adjusted his tie. Brady stood six feet tall and weighed two hundred pounds. His blonde ponytail stopped at the middle of his back. Brady favored the NFL superstar Ben Roethlisberger.

Millie stepped out into the backyard dressed in an expensive looking navy blue skirt suit. On her feet was a pair of navy blue heels. On her face was a pair of oversized shades. Bringing up her rear was Nicole and Knuckles.

"Hey, Brady. It's a pleasure to meet you," Millie smiled as her and Brady shook hands.

"Please have a seat," Brady said as he openly checked Millie out. "I have to say you look amazing."

"Thank you."

"Now, how can I help you?" Brady sat down and crossed his legs.

"I'm looking for a steady connect," Millie began. "Someone who can deliver a shit load of product. I have a crazy demand. All I'm lacking is the supply."

"How much supply are you looking for?" Brady asked curiously.

"I need at least two hundred bricks a month."

Brady chuckled. "You can't be serious." He took another sip from his drink. "Do you have the funds to cover two hundred a month?"

"I'm good for it," Millie said quickly.

"Listen, Millie. I know you didn't come all the way out to Miami to waste my time?" Brady asked.

"Give me the two hundred and I'll have your money for you in three weeks," Millie stated plainly.

"Three weeks is a quick turnaround, Millie." Brady stood to his feet. "Let's say I give you the two hundred bricks and you don't have my money in three weeks. Then what?"

"Then you can kill me and my entire family," was Millie's response. Millie knew a man of Brady's status didn't play when it came to his money and she wanted to let him know that she was serious about her business.

Brady chuckled again. "I like how you do business," he said. He liked people who believed in themselves. "I like your style, Millie," Brady paused. "So I'll tell you what I'm going to do. I'm going to give you the two hundred bricks and you have three weeks to get me back my money," he paused to take a sip from his drink. "But for whatever reason I don't get my money…I'm sure you already know what the outcome will be."

"Thank you for believing in me, Brady, and I promise I won't let you down," Millie stood and extended her hand. Brady grabbed her hand and kissed the back of it gently.

"Millie, I look forward to doing business with you for a very long time," Brady smiled.

"Are you this nice to all of your customers?" Millie flirted back.

"None of them look like you," Brady admitted. "I'm trusting you and I don't trust a lot of people. Please don't let me down, Millie."

Knuckles stood on the sideline ice grilling Brady. He didn't like the way he was looking at Millie and openly checking her out but he knew that this meeting was a big deal for Millie so he decided to remain cool.

"When you get back to New York go down to Times Square. There will be an old school hooptie in front of Applebee's. The keys will be on top of the back tire and in the trunk is where all the product will be stored. Call me when you made the pick up and be safe," Brady said.

"Will do and thanks again for the opportunity," Millie said humbly as she and her crew made their exit. Once Millie was out of war shot, Slim spoke up. "You think she's going to be able to pull it off in three weeks?"

"For her and her family's sake, I hope so," Brady said.

The Black Dragon

Seventeen

The Black Dragon sat behind the wheel of a tinted out black Yukon as he followed Eric's Range Rover. He had been trailing Eric's every last move for the last four days and figured today was the best time for him to strike. It was a rainy and nasty day, which meant that there wouldn't be a lot of police around. The Black Dragon made sure he stayed four lengths behind the Range Rover. All the rain made it a little easier for the Black Dragon to fly under the radar. On the Black Dragon's lap sat a tech-9. His windshield wipers worked in overtime as he watched the Range Rover come to a stop at a fancy steakhouse.

***

Eric sat in the back seat of the Range Rover looking over some paperwork on a new investment property he was thinking about purchasing. "These numbers are pretty good," Eric said out loud, as he stuffed the papers back inside the manila envelope. "Any word on where the Russo family is hiding out?"

Pistol Pete shook his head. "Nah but I'm sure they still have something up their sleeves. I spoke to Jimmy and he said that he has a whole crew of his men out looking for anyone associated with the Russo family."

"Cool, keep me posted on that situation," Eric said as he stepped out of the back seat of the Range Rover. Immediately, one of his bodyguards opened an umbrella and held it over Eric's head, protecting him from the rain. Pistol Pete and the rest of Eric's security quickly formed a circle around him as they escorted him inside the restaurant.

Eric stepped in the restaurant and immediately he spotted his mother sitting in the back along with the big beast, Knuckles. Eric made his way to the back of the restaurant and helped himself to a seat. "Why the hell didn't you tell me that Nicole was an assassin?" he huffed in a strong whisper.

"What difference does it make?" Millie said not bothering to look up from her plate. "Y'all were both attracted to one another and y'all made each other happy. That's all that matters."

"Bullshit!" Eric yelled causing other diners to nosily look over in their direction. "You are supposed to be my mother and a mother is supposed to protect their child. Not hook them up with a crazy killer!"

"Great, so tell the entire restaurant," Millie said unmoved. She knew why Eric was upset but there was nothing she could do about it now. "Son, while I was away I was worried about you so I hooked you up with Nicole so she could protect you since I couldn't at the time," Millie said laying it on thick. "I know you are upset but you know that girl loves you." she looked up in Eric's eyes. "She told me she risked her own life to save yours."

Eric nodded. "Yeah, she did." He loved Nicole to death but he just felt betrayed and left in the dark with the whole situation. Eric hated finding out things last. Especially something about his woman.

"I know sometimes you don't understand the things that I do but that's why I'm the parent," Millie took a sip from her glass of wine. "And some things aren't meant for you to understand."

"From now on I'm going to need you to be straight up with me!" Eric huffed.

"Go see Nicole and make everything right," Millie shoveled a piece of steak in her mouth. "Go get your girl back and get out my face bothering me before I give you a spanking like I used to do when you were a kid," she laughed. "She's staying at one of Frank Russo's hotels a few blocks away from the mansion."

"Why is she staying there?" Eric asked with his face crumbled up. Just Frank's name alone rubbed him the wrong way.

"She didn't want to stay in your hotel and upset you so I advised her to stay at that hotel," Millie shrugged. "She had to stay somewhere."

Eric stood to his feet, kissed Millie on the cheek, and got ready to leave when Millie grabbed his arm and stopped him. "Sit down; I called you here for a reason." Millie took another sip from her glass of wine. "I got the faucet put back on."

"Word? How did you make that happen?" Eric said with a shocked look on his face. While Millie was away, Eric had tried to score product from every wholesaler out there with no luck. "Who's supplying us?"

"Brady," Millie said with a smile.

"You mean crazy Brady out in Miami?" Eric asked with a raised brow. Eric had heard plenty of stories about Brady and they were all violent and ended with someone either dying or never being heard from or seen again. "Please be careful while you're dealing with him."

"I'm not worried about that," Millie said quickly. "My concern is getting rid of all this product."

Eric noticed a certain look in his mother's eyes and immediately knew that something was wrong. "What did you do?"

"I took a whole lot of product and I have three weeks to get rid of it," Millie said in a cool tone as if she had everything under control. "We're having a family meeting at the house tonight at eight. Don't be late."

"I won't," Eric said as stood and turned to head for the exit. Once outside, Eric's bodyguards quickly formed a circle around him trying to shield him from any type of danger. Just as Eric lifted, one leg to step up inside the Range Rover one of his bodyguard's head exploded like a melon sending blood and brain matter all over Eric's face. Immediately, Eric was tackled down to the ground by one of his bodyguards. Pistol Pete quickly took cover behind a parked car and returned fire on the gunman.

The Black Dragon held his finger down on the trigger of his machine gun as he moved forward shooting anything moving. He quickly reloaded his weapon as he watched one of the bodyguards toss Eric in the back of the SUV.

Pistol Pete quickly jumped behind the wheel, threw the gear in reverse, and stomped down on the gas pedal. The Black Dragon opened fire on the Range Rover. He watched as his bullets cracked the front windshield but didn't penetrate.

"Stay down!" Pistol Pete yelled with his arm behind the passenger seat's headrest as he listened to the machine gun bullets smash into the bulletproof windshield as the Range Rover tires screeched loudly.

The Black Dragon chased after the Range Rover until the vehicle finally bent the corner.

***

Millie sat in the restaurant finishing up her steak when she heard the loud sound of machine gun fire. She quickly shot to her feet and stormed towards the exit with Knuckles close on her heels. Millie immediately thought the worst when she heard the thunderous shots. Her hand shot down inside her purse and came out carrying a .380. Millie pushed the restaurant door open and saw the Black Dragon running down the street with a machine gun in his hand. Millie aimed her gun at the assassin but held back on pulling the trigger when she saw the two cop cars in pursuit of the Black Dragon. With all of her legal troubles, she figured it would be best to just allow the authorities to take care of it. Millie slipped her gun back down in her purse as she noticed three of Eric's bodyguards laid out on the concrete in a pool of their own blood.

"Come on, Millie. We have to go," Knuckles said as he gently placed his hand on her back noticing several cop cars pulling up to a screeching stop. "Eric is fine."

***

The Black Dragon spun around the corner and dashed inside a high priced clothing store. He pushed several women down to the floor as he ran towards the back exit. The Black Dragon busted through the staircase door and paused when he realized that the back door was locked. The Black Dragon spun around and shot the first cop dead with a head shot. He quickly dashed up the stairs as the police opened fire on him trying to take his head off. The Black Dragon turned the corner as several bullets lodged in the wall right where his head was just a second ago. The Black Dragon recklessly fired a few shots over his shoulder just to buy him some time and keep the cops at bay as he continued on to the roof.

Several cops cautiously made their way up to the roof. On a silent count of three, one of the cops snatched the door open as the rest of the cops ran out onto the roof with their guns drawn only to find the roof empty.

Nicole

Eighteen

Nicole laid on the bed in her hotel room staring up at the ceiling while The Weekend's voice hummed smoothly through the small speakers. For the last two days, she kept herself cooped up in the room and away from the real world. All that was on Nicole's mind was Eric. A part of her still couldn't believe that Eric had actually dumped her and kicked her out because she saved his life. The more Nicole thought about it the more she wanted to march over to Eric's mansion and kick his ass for treating her like this. "That motherfucker got some nerve," Nicole huffed as she turned over on her side and prepared to take a nap. Lately sleep seemed to be the only way for Nicole to get her mind to stop thinking. Nicole closed her eyes as she heard light knock at the door. Nicole's hand quickly shot under the pillow as she grabbed her P-90 and slowly headed to the door. Nicole looked through the peephole then lowered her gun. She took a deep breath before she cracked the door and stuck her head out. "What do you want? And how did you find me?"

Eric stood on the other side of the door holding a dozen roses in his hand. "We need to talk."

"We don't have nothing to talk about," Nicole shot back quickly. "The other night I think you said more than enough."

"Baby, can I please come in so we can talk?"

Nicole opened the door an inch further and walked back inside the room helping herself to a seat on the bed. "Talk!" she snapped. "And whatever comes out of your mouth better be damn good."

"Well, I just came by to bring you these," Eric handed Nicole the roses. "And I wanted to tell you that I'm sorry for the way I spoke and treated you."

"Hmmp," Nicole huffed.

"Also I came over here to ask if you would please come back home," Eric asked.

"Why so you can kick me out again?" Nicole asked, being smart. On the outside, her face still looked as if she had an attitude but on the inside, she was happy to see Eric. As Nicole sat listening to Eric, every few seconds she would sniff her roses.

"Baby, I apologize. I just don't like being left in the dark especially when it comes to my woman," Eric admitted. "If it wasn't for you I'd probably be dead right now."

"Probably my ass!" Nicole huffed. "If I wasn't there you would have definitely been dead."

"Is there anything I can do to repay you?" Eric moved in closer. He stood one inch away from her face. "And when I say anything," he paused and licked his lips. "I mean anything,"

Nicole stood up on her tippy toes and kissed Eric like she had just been released from doing a five-year bid in prison. "What's this?" Nicole looked down and saw dry specs of blood on the collar of his shirt.

"Oh, that ain't nothing. Just had another run in with the Black Dragon today," Eric said trying to downplay the situation. Nicole pushed Eric out of her space. "Why the hell didn't you call me?"

"Everything happened so fast." Eric moved in and cupped both of Nicole's ass cheeks. "I don't want to talk about that. I want to focus on us getting back into a good space."

Nicole leaned in to kiss Eric when she heard a loud knock at the door.

"You expecting company or something?" Eric asked with a hint of jealousy in his voice.

"Nah, the only person that even knows I'm here is Millie." Nicole headed to the door to see who was interrupting her and Eric's moment. Nicole opened the door and out in the hallway stood three big Italian men dressed in suits. "Can I help you?"

"Ma'am, step to the side. We're here to get the man in your room off the property," the leader of the pack spoke in a deep voice.

"What's the problem?" Nicole asked, suddenly remembering that they were in a Russo hotel.

"Step to the side, ma'am," the leader said forcing his way inside the room. He held a metal baton in his hand. The leader took another step, when his feet were quickly swept from under him. Eric watched as the big man hit the floor hard. Nicole caught the next man in the room with a quick rabbit punch that stunned him. She quickly followed up with a knee to the man's stomach then proceeded to roughly take the man down to the floor. The third man hit Nicole in the back with his baton when Eric ran full speed and tackled him down to the floor out into the hallway. Eric looked up and saw Pistol Pete getting busy with two Italian men at the end of the hall. The big man punched Eric in the face then picked him up and violently slammed him down to the floor. The big man handled Eric. The big man picked Eric up, ran full speed, and rammed Eric's back into the wall.

Back in the room, Nicole stood behind the big Italian man and snapped his neck. Nicole ran over to the bed and removed her pistol. She screwed the silencer on the barrel as she stepped out into the hallway with fire dancing in her eyes. Nicole walked up to the two men that Pistol Pete was fighting with and put a bullet in the back of both of their heads. Nicole then headed towards the staircase where Eric and the last Italian man stood going blow for blow. Neither one backing down or letting up in either man's eye. The Italian man weaved Eric's last punch, scooped him off his feet, and tossed him down the stairs as if he was a rag doll. The Italian man stood at the top of the stairs with a smile of victory on his face when out of nowhere his brains popped out the top of his head. The Italian man's body crumbled down to the floor then tumbled down the stairs. Nicole stood behind him holding a smoking gun in her hand. Her face covered with specs of blood. "Come on, baby! We have to go!" Nicole ran down the steps and quickly helped Eric to his feet.

Jimmy Mason
Nineteen

"Let me get that for you, baby." Jimmy stepped out of the driver seat and walked around to the passenger side, opened the door, and watched as Cherokee stepped out dressed in a tight fitting purple dress with the purple heels to match. Her hair was freshly done and her makeup was flawless. For the last few weeks, Jimmy had been in the doghouse and couldn't seem to keep Cherokee off his back so tonight he decided to take her out to a nice restaurant and wine and dine her. He hoped that would get him back on her good side. "You look amazing, baby."

"Mm…hmm," Cherokee huffed. She knew exactly what Jimmy was up to and wasn't falling for his games. "And don't think just because you're taking me out that you getting some of this good pussy later either."

"Ain't nobody thinking about you or that box right now," Jimmy lied. "I'm just trying to take my queen out and have a nice time."

"Oh, so now I'm your queen?" Cherokee rolled her eyes. "Was I your queen when you had that light skin girl all up in your face at the club the other night? Was I your queen then?"

"You always going to be my queen," Jimmy wrapped his arm around Cherokee's waist as they entered the restaurant. The hostess escorted the couple to a nice candle lit table. Over in the middle of the floor sat a man in a nice suit playing a soft tune on the piano.

"This place is nice," Cherokee smiled, as the waiter brought a bottle of red wine and sat it on their table along with two wine glasses.

"Need a little bit more time to look over the menu?" the waiter asked politely.

"Yeah give us a minute," Jimmy quickly dismissed the waiter and turned his focus back on Cherokee. He reached under the table and rubbed on Cherokee's leg but she quickly smacked his hand away.

"Get your hands off me. Ain't no telling where they been," Cherokee spat as she lifted her glass up to her mouth and took a deep sip of wine. "And what you in such a good mood for?"

"My moms just texted me," Jimmy smiled. "The faucet just got put back on so we're back in business."

Cherokee huffed. "Guess that means I won't be seeing you much," she said with a slight attitude. Cherokee knew how busy Jimmy was going to be in the upcoming weeks but she didn't complain, especially since it was drug money that allowed her to live such a lavish lifestyle.

"Yeah, I'm about to put the streets back in a head lock," Jimmy boasted. As Jimmy spoke, Cherokee noticed four Italian men quickly making their way over to their table over Jimmy's shoulder.

"Baby, I think we got company," Cherokee whispered.

"How many?" Jimmy slipped his hand inside his suit jacket and gripped the handle of his 9mm. He made sure not to look back not wanting to alert his attackers.

"Four," Cherokee answered.

***

Bad News stepped inside the fancy restaurant with a no-nonsense look on his face and a baseball bat in his hand. Behind him were three of his toughest goons who also carried baseball bats. Bad News walked swiftly through the restaurant until he spotted Jimmy and some big booty girl sitting down having a conversation over a glass of wine. Before Jimmy could get the heads up, Bad News jogged towards the couple's table and hit Jimmy in the back of the head with the baseball bat. The wooden bat echoed loudly as it bounced off the back of Jimmy's skull. Jimmy fell out his chair and clutched the back of his head. He dropped his gun in the process of him falling to the floor.

"Yeah, talk that shit now motherfucker!" Bad News growled as he and his comrades beat Jimmy down with their bats as if he was a dog in the streets.

Cherokee snatched the wine bottle off the table and shattered it over one of the Italian men head. She was quickly rewarded with a backslap that took her off her feet. Bad News picked up the table and lifted it over his head then violently tossed it down on Cherokee. Bad News then dragged Cherokee's body and laid it on top of Jimmy. "I have a message from Frank Russo." Bad News pulled out his penis and peed on both Jimmy and Cherokee. "Maybe next time you'll think twice about fucking with a don," Bad News laughed as him and his team exited the restaurant.

Millie Mason
Twenty

Millie sat at the head of the table with an annoyed look on her face. "Okay, looks like we're going to have to get this meeting started without Jimmy." She paused for a second to take a sip of water. "Like I told everyone, we are back in business and it's time to take the streets back over. Of course, we know Mike is no longer with us anymore which means we have to move a lot smarter. We have three weeks to get this money back to Brady so we don't have no time to play no games. I need everyone on their A game."

"I have all the stash houses lined up and ready to go," Eric said.

Murder sat at the table with a concerned look on his face. He had called Jimmy over ten times with no answer or reply. "I got all the soldiers lined up and ready to go. The streets are hungry right now."

"Then let's feed them," Millie said. "Each crew will be supplied tonight. Let's put the Mason family name back on the map." Millie paused when she smelled something burning. "Y'all smell that?" Millie stood to her feet and grabbed her .380 from her holster. She walked out to the back to inspect where the smell was coming from. Millie stepped out back and saw a hooded man hunched over holding a container of gasoline in his hand. Without warning, Millie shot the hooded man in the back three times. She stepped over the hooded man's dead body and worked her way around to the other side of the house where she saw bright orange and blue flames. "Shit!" Millie cursed as she saw the side of the house going up in flames. As Millie stood admiring the flames, she was suddenly tackled down to the ground from behind. She rolled over and struggled with the next hooded man. While Millie rolled around on the ground with the mystery man she heard several gunshots being fired coming somewhere from the other side of the mansion. Eric ran out the back door in search of his mother and found her rolling on the ground with a hooded man. Eric quickly put a bullet in the back of the hooded man's head then helped his mother back up to her feet. "There's four more men on the other side of the house!" Eric said as he led Millie back inside the mansion.

Meanwhile, on the other side of the mansion, Lethal Weapon broke into a side door and entered the mansion like a cat burglar. He immediately splashed gasoline on anything he laid his eyes on. Without thinking twice, Lethal Weapon struck a match, tossed it over his shoulder, and moved on to the next part of the house. Lethal Weapon stepped over several dead bodies as he left a long trail of gasoline on the floor. Some of the bodies belonged to the Mason family security while the others were good friends of Lethal Weapon. Lethal Weapon stopped when he looked ahead and saw four security guards headed his way. He quickly struck a match, set the rest of the mansion on fire, and then took off in a sprint down the hall.

Pistol Pete stopped short as the flames rose to eye level. He raised his arm and sent five shots at Lethal Weapon's departing back. "Fuck!" Pistol Pete cursed, as he headed back downstairs.

***

Nicole sprang from behind the wall and dropped two hooded men with headshots. She stepped over the dead bodies and kneeled down and touched the pulse of one of the Mason family's favorite security guards only to find out there wasn't one. "Damn." Nicole stood back to her feet and continued on through the mansion. She wanted to save as many of her people as possible. As Nicole moved throughout the mansion, she stopped when she felt a strong hand reach out and grab her ankle. She looked down and saw a hooded man begging for some assistance. Nicole aimed her gun at the man's face and pulled the trigger with no remorse. Then she backpedaled outside.

Millie stood in front of the driveway and watched as the mansion burned. Her clothes were covered in blood and her nails were ruined. Millie turned to Eric. "I want to know who's responsible for this by the morning," she said in a light whisper. Knuckles walked over and placed a friendly hand on Millie's shoulder. "I'm sorry the house is burning."

"It's not your fault," Millie replied in a whisper. Then she turned to Murder. "I need you to go and find Jimmy now and tell him to call me immediately!"

Lethal Weapon
Twenty-One

Lethal Weapon laid in his bed staring at the ceiling. The scene of the Mason family mansion burning down replayed in his mind repeatedly. Every time he thought about it, a small sick smile crept on his face. Lethal Weapon loved to use violence to solve any and every problem and was thrilled when Frank Russo gave him the green light to go at the Mason family. Not only was Lethal Weapon doing something he loved he was also getting paid for it. Lethal Weapon's thoughts were interrupted when he heard his alarm system go off, followed by the sound of a grown man howling in pain. "What the hell?" Lethal Weapon sat up, grabbed his .45 from off the nightstand, and headed downstairs to investigate what had triggered off the alarm. He made it downstairs and saw two of his closest friends sprawled out on the floor with a bullet lodged in the middle of both of their foreheads. Friends that he'd done time with; friends that he trusted with his life. Now, Lethal Weapon would have to come up with a lie to tell their mother's. Lethal Weapon took a few steps forward then came to a sudden stop when he heard movement coming from behind him.

"Drop that gun right now!" Nicole growled in a light whisper. "Don't make me repeat myself," she warned. Lethal Weapon slowly placed his gun down on the floor and turned around so he could look his killer in the eyes.

"A woman, a fucking woman! You gotta be kidding me!" Lethal Weapon laughed. "After all the wrong I've done all my life, this is how it's going to end, huh? Me getting killed by a woman!"

"Millie Mason sends her love," Nicole said then pulled the trigger shooting Lethal Weapon dead in the face. She didn't even bother to wait around to see his body hit the floor.

***

Eric sat in the car with a nervous look on his face. He felt bad for sending Nicole into the house all by herself but she begged and insisted on him letting her handle everything on her own. The longer Nicole remained inside the property the more nervous Eric became and the more he had to talk himself out running up in the house like a mad man. As a man, he felt as if he was supposed to be the one fighting for the family. Not his woman. Eric glanced down at his watch. "If she ain't out in one minute, I'm going in there," he said to himself. A 9mm rested on Eric's lap with a silencer attached to the barrel. Millie told him that Nicole was the best but Eric still didn't see her as an assassin. Instead, he saw her as the love of his life. He was used to her cooking, washing dishes, and looking sexy. Not kicking ass and holding guns. "Fuck this!" Eric growled as opened the driver door. But before his foot could even touch the ground, he looked up and saw Nicole walk out the front door and down the path toward the truck. She slid in the passenger seat, put on her seat belt, and leaned over and kissed Eric on the cheek. "Come on, let's get out of here."

Eric quickly shifted the gear in drive and pulled away from the curb. For the first two minutes of the ride, neither Eric nor Nicole said a word until finally Eric decided to break the ice. "So, how did it go back there?"

"That was a piece of cake," Nicole said nonchalantly.

"So like…how did you get started?" Eric asked.

"In what? The cleaning business?"

"Yeah."

"Well, let me start off by saying I used to be a good girl once upon a time but lack of money will make you do some things one may not have known they were even capable of doing," Nicole said. "I did my first job when I was fourteen," she admitted. "I didn't have any money and a guy offered to pay me $3,000 to kill someone." Nicole paused for a second. "I was desperate and needed the money so I said "what the hell." Then, after that job, I did another and then another until finally I decided to take it seriously. I began training my body as well as my mind. I practiced on my aim for years, worked on hand to hand combat, and became a beast."

Eric sat with his mouth wide-open taking in every word.

"Being in the line of work I'm in, it wasn't smart for me to be in a relationship," Nicole explained. "I'm no virgin but this is most definitely my first real relationship and when you dumped me a few weeks ago I felt so empty and alone." Nicole paused to wipe a tear from her eye. "I realized at that moment that I would give it all up just to be with you."

Her words hit Eric hard and made him feel bad for dumping her. He had no idea the type of hurt she had been through in her life. All he saw was a pretty face and a nice body. He was now learning about Nicole's history and it only made him love her even more. Eric placed his hand on top of Nicole's. "I never meant to hurt you, baby."

Nicole nodded. "I know, baby. Pull over right here."

"Right here?" Eric asked. They were on the highway going seventy miles per hour.

"Yes, right here!"

"Thinking it was an emergency," Eric quickly signaled and pulled over to the shoulder of the road. When the truck came to a stop, Nicole quickly hopped out. Eric got out along with Nicole and walked around to the passenger side to see what was wrong. "What's the matter?"

Nicole stood there for a second looking into Eric's eyes not saying a word. Without warn, Nicole dropped down to one knee and removed a jewelry box from her pocket. "Eric, will you marry me?" Nicole opened the jewelry revealing a diamond encrusted wedding band.

Eric stood there with his mouth wide open at a loss for words. He couldn't believe what his ears were hearing. Never in a million years would he have expected this. "Are you serious?"

Nicole nodded looking up into Eric's eyes.

"Yes! Of course, I'll marry you," Eric smiled as Nicole slid the ring on his finger. He grabbed Nicole and pulled her in close as the two locked lips.

"I don't ever want to be without you," Nicole whispered.

"And you never have to, baby."

Murder

Twenty-Two

Murder pulled into Jimmy's driveway and killed the engine. It had been a couple of days since the last time he had spoken to or heard from Jimmy so Murder took it upon himself to just pop up at Jimmy's house and see what was really going on. Not knowing what to expect, Murder gripped the handle of his 9mm and rang the doorbell. A few seconds later, Cherokee answered the door. "Oh hey, Murder. Come on in."

Murder stepped inside the lavish home and the first thing he noticed was the huge gash just above Cherokee's eye. "Everything alright?" Murder nodded towards the gash on Cherokee's face. "I've been trying to call Jimmy for the last few days and I got no answer."

"Yeah, my bad. We got into a little scuffle the other night with some Italian clowns," Cherokee said as if the beating she and Jimmy had taken was nothing. "Come on, he's right back here."

Murder stepped in the room and saw Jimmy laying in the bed looking all battered and bruised. "What the fuck happen?"

"A group of Italian men ran down on me and Cherokee and attacked us with baseball bats," Jimmy shrugged as if it wasn't a big deal. His head was wrapped in bandages and his eyes were black and blue.

"Why you ain't call me?"

"I must have lost my phone during the fight," Jimmy shrugged as if it wasn't a big deal. "I'll be out of action for about a week or two but as soon as I'm back I'll definitely be paying those Italian fucks a visit."

"Don't even worry about it, big bro. I'll take care of those fucks for you," Murder volunteered. It hurt him to see Jimmy laid up in the bed all beat up.

"Do what you gotta do. Just make sure you save some action for me," Jimmy smiled.

"No doubt," Murder smiled as he turned and made his exit.

Twenty-Three

S o, we looking good?" Millie asked with her iPhone pressed up against her ear. She sat in the passenger seat of her black Yukon. "Listen, I don't care about all that. Tell him I need to use his crib as a stash point. Blank. Period." Millie growled. "Listen, tell him if I have to come up there it's not going to be pretty," she hung up in the caller's ear.

"Everything alright?" Knuckles asked, keeping his eyes on the road.

"Yeah, I'm good. Pull over right here," Millie ordered. Once the SUV came to a stop, Millie stepped out of the truck and entered the bodega that sat on the corner with Knuckles close on her heels. Millie stepped in the store and waited patiently for the last customer to leave before she headed to the counter. "Mike, I've been calling. Why haven't you returned any of my calls?"

"Oh hey, Millie," Mike said with a nervous look in his eyes. "My bad, I been so busy. How you been? You looking good."

"Mike, you're making a lot of money out of this store and I need in," Millie said getting straight to the point. "I have some pure A-1 uncut shit and I need you to pump it for me."

SILK WHITE

"Sorry, Millie but I'm kind of working with someone else," Mike said nervously.

"Who?"

"Some cat named Maniac," Mike answered. "When you left he came in and flooded the city with coke."

"Well, he must not be doing too much because I never heard of him," Millie said.

"I would love to work for you, Millie. Besides, you've always been fair with the pay. This guy, Maniac, pays all of his workers peanuts," Mike said. "I just don't want any problems with Maniac so if you could maybe talk to him and let him know that I'll be working for you from now on that would be great."

"Don't worry about Maniac. I'll take care of him," Millie replied. "You know where I can find him?"

Mike quickly scribbled an address down on a sheet of paper then slid it over to Millie. "Here's where you can find him."

Millie took the paper and handed it to Knuckles. "I'll call you first thing in the morning," she yelled over her shoulder as her and Knuckles exited the bodega.

Back in the truck, Knuckles merged onto the highway then glared over at Millie. "So, what's the plan?"

"We going to go over there and talk to Maniac and make him an offer he can't refuse," Millie answered. "Have you heard of anything from this Maniac?"

"Yeah, I heard he's an OG and one of the leaders of the Bloods organization," Knuckles said. "He has an army of young stupid Bloods ready to kill for him at a drop of a hat."

"He'd be perfect if we could recruit him and get him on our team," Millie thought aloud. With a guy like Maniac on the team, Millie knew that the sky was the limit.

"I don't know. I heard that Maniac is a real loose cannon and very disrespectful," Knuckles added. "I never met him in person but I've heard stories."

Knuckles pulled up in front of a project building and placed the gear in park. "This is the address."

Millie stepped out the truck and entered the projects. It was a fairly nice night out so the projects were alive and full of movement. Millie and Knuckles strolled through the projects looking for the building number that was scribbled down on the paper that Mike had given them.

"I think that's him over there," Knuckles nodded over towards a crowd of men huddled up by the flagpole rolling dice. Millie approached the men who were all dressed in some kind of red attire.

"Hey. I'm looking for Maniac," Millie said loud enough for the group of men to hear her.

At the sound of her voice, all the men quickly spun around to see whom the voice belonged to. "Who the fuck is this bitch?" one of the men spat ignorantly.

"I said I'm looking for Maniac," Millie repeated in a firm tone. A slim muscular cat with a lot of tattoos stepped forward.

"Look bitch," he barked. "You in the wrong neighborhood asking the wrong questions so I suggest you get the fuck up out of here before something bad happens to you," he said coldly.

"And who am I speaking with?" Millie asked politely.

"Big Blood!" the man said as he pounded on his chest for extra emphasis.

"Well listen, Big Blood," Millie said making air quotes with her fingers. "My name is Millie Mason and I ain't going nowhere until I speak to Maniac!"

Big Blood slowly removed his shirt and tossed it over on the bench. "Look, bitch!" he growled with a finger pointed in Millie's face. "I just told you to get up out of here before you and your retarded friend here gets fucked up!"

As soon as Knuckles heard the word "retard," he snapped. With the swiftness of a cat and the power of a lion, he swung a powerful hook. Big Blood ducked the punch just in time and watched as the powerful punch connected with the jaw of the man standing next to him instantly putting him to sleep. Big Blood and the rest of the Bloods quickly jumped on Knuckles like a pack of alley cats. It took about twenty men to finally get Knuckles off his feet. Millie removed a small knife from her purse, ran over, and stabbed a few of the Blood members before she was blindsided from behind and knocked out cold.

Eric
Twenty-Four

Eric sat in his office sipping on a cup of coffee as he paced back and forth. It had been forty-eight hours since he'd last heard from his mother and he was beginning to think the worst. "Still no word from her?" Eric asked when Pistol Pete entered the office.

"Not yet. I got Nicole out looking for her now," Pistol Pete replied.

"Yeah, I just spoke to Nicole and she hasn't heard anything either," Eric huffed. At the moment, the only thing good going for the Mason family was that the streets were buzzing about the new product that Brady provided them with.

"Brady came through with that fire," Pistol Pete said. "Streets been loving this shit."

"Facts," Eric replied quickly. "Any word on the Black Dragon?"

"Nah, it's been real quiet."

Eric knew that just because the Black Dragon hadn't shown his face in a while, it didn't mean that their beef over and he wasn't about to let his guard down. Eric sat on the edge of his desk when he heard his cell phone vibrating across the desk. "Yo," he answered.

"Hey, baby. It's me," Nicole's voice sounded a little nervous.

"What's wrong, baby?" Eric asked sensing that something was wrong.

"I tracked your mother's phone like you asked me to do and it led me to some raggedy looking warehouse," Nicole said, as she scoped the place out from her car. "From the looks of it, this seems to be one of the Bloods meeting spots because there's about a million of them out here."

"So, you think my mother is in there?"

"It's definitely possible," Nicole countered as she noticed a red Range Rover pull up in front of the warehouse. Out stepped a tall handsome dark skin man who wore all black with a pair of red Converse on his feet. Hanging out of the man's right back pocket rested a crisp red bandana. Nicole didn't know who the man was but whoever he was, she knew he was important from how all of the other Blood members suddenly got in line when he showed up. "I don't know what's going on but I'm about to go and check it out."

"No, wait until your back up gets there," Eric demanded.

"No time. I'm going in." Nicole ended the call.

"Shit!" Eric cursed as he grabbed his keys and ran out the door.

**

Millie woke up in some sort of dirty warehouse. On the floor next to her was Knuckles. He laid on the floor next to her badly beaten and all bruised up. "You alright, baby," she whispered as she reached out and rubbed his head. Knuckles wasn't able to speak due to the broken jaw he received so all he could do was nod his head. "Don't worry. I'm going to get us out of this," Millie said then slowly stood to her feet. She was immediately met by Big Blood.

"Where am I?" Millie asked. She looked around the warehouse looking for an escape route. Without warning, Big Blood slapped the shit out of her.

"You don't speak unless you're spoken to!" Big Blood growled.

"What the fuck is going on in here!" a voice boomed and immediately everything stopped. Maniac stepped in the warehouse flanked by four rough-faced goons. "What have we here?" Maniac said as he approached the battered and bruised woman.

"This bitch came to the block talking about she wanted to speak with you," Big Blood explain. "I told her to bounce and her big goofy friend here swung on me."

"Speak your peace," Maniac said, looking Millie up and down.

"My name is Millie Mason and I came here to talk business with you," Millie explained. "Me and my family used to control all the real estate out here on these streets but when I went away on a little vacation things changed," she said. "But now I'm back and I have a smoking product and I'm willing to give you prices you can't refuse."

"I appreciate you coming here to talk business with me," Maniac said politely. "And I apologize about what happened to your friend here," he nodded towards Knuckles. "But I already have a solid connect."

"Listen, Maniac. I really need you as a partner because I need my real estate back and I'd rather partner with you instead of going to war with you," Millie stated plainly. "We can both walk away winners and no one has to get hurt."

Maniac smiled. "I've heard a lot of wild stories about you and the Mason family when I was younger. I always wanted to work for your family."

"Well, now is your chance." Millie smiled. "Work with me and I'll forget about all this nonsense that has taken place."

"I would love to work with you but unfortunately I can't," Maniac said. "I already have an agreement with my connect.

But I would like to make this up to you so we don't have any bad blood." Maniac knew that going to war with the Mason family would be horrible for business so if there was a way for him to squash any differences they had between one another, that's what he planned on doing.

"I like how you handled this so there won't be no hard feelings. I'll just chalk this up as a misunderstanding," Millie extended her hand. She liked how he had handled the situation and respected his straightforwardness. Maniac smiled and reached out to shake Millie's hand when a bullet exploded in his shoulder dropping him instantly.

Big Blood looked on in shock as he watched several members from his organization drop like flies. He and the rest of his team quickly took cover and opened fire in the direction of the gunman.

***

Nicole held a two handed grip on her gun as she dropped four of the gang members with headshots. She moved through the warehouse like a ghost hiding behind the shadows using her pinpoint accuracy to kill as many gang members as possible.

Once Millie saw the gang members start to drop like flies, she quickly grabbed Knuckles and made a dash towards the exit. Millie didn't see Nicole but she knew that this was definitely her work. Once Nicole saw that Millie was out of the warehouse safely she tossed a smoke bomb towards the middle of the warehouse then took off in a sprint as the sound of multiple guns being fired at the same time went off loudly. Nicole made it around the corner just as several bullets ricocheted loudly off the wall.

Outside, Millie and Knuckles ran until a black Range Rover came to a screeching stop in front of them. The driver window rolled down and Eric stuck his head out. "Come on! Come on! Come on!" Millie and Knuckles quickly piled up in the back seat.

"Where's Nicole?" Eric asked in a panic.

"I don't know but we gotta go!" Millie said only thinking about herself. Eric got ready to pull off when he saw Nicole burst around the corner in a full sprint. Her chest heaved up and down as her arms and legs worked overtime. Millie opened the back door and Nicole dove into the backseat. Once Eric was sure that everyone was in the truck safely, he stomped down on the gas pedal. The tires burnt rubber as the sound of bullets pinging loudly off the truck could be heard. Eric made sure to keep his head down until he finally made it to the highway.

Derrick Mason
Twenty-Five

D errick Mason sat in the day room playing chess with his cellmate, a big muscular man that went by the name Butter. During their chess game, Butter was filling Derrick in on what was going on out in the streets. "Yeah, I heard it's an all-out war going on out in the streets between the Mason family and the Bloods," Butter said, as he made his move on the chessboard. "Heard Millie shot one of the big homies. Some OG named Maniac."

"Are you serious?" Derrick asked with his face crumbled up. It seemed like every other week the Mason family was beefing with a powerful organization. All Derrick could do was shake his head. While he was home and in charge the Mason family never had this many problems. "My wife is a problem magnet."

"Yeah, well, if shit jumps off in here just know I got your back," Butter said strongly. "We brothers so whatever they do to you they gon have to do to me first!" he roared.

"You mean that?"

"No doubt!" Butter answered.

"Good, because there's four of them headed in our direction right now," Derrick said looking down at the chessboard trying to make it seem like he hadn't noticed them coming.

"Wha...what? Right now?" Butter stuttered, his tough guy persona now gone. The tough look on his face was now replaced with one of fear. Derrick reached down in his shoe and removed the four-inch blade that he had been sharpening for occasions just like this.

"Just be cool and follow my lead," Derrick said in a calm tone. The four Blood members reached the table and stood over both Derrick and Butter. Derrick slowly looked up from the chessboard. "Something I can help you gentlemen with?"

"Yeah, what's poppin. We need to have a quick word with you," the leader of the pack spoke with venom in his tone.

"I would love to speak with you all but right now I'm in the middle of a game," Derrick nodded down at the chessboard. Butter sat there quietly. He looked as if at any second he was going to shit himself.

"Nigga, fuck this game!" the leader of the pack barked as he slapped all the chess pieces on the floor. "I said I need to talk to you right now, motherfucker!"

Twenty-Six

"Nigga fuck this game!" the leader of the pack barked as he slapped all the chest pieces on the floor. "I said I need to talk to you right now, motherfucker!"

Derrick played it off as if he was about to cooperate, then in one swift motion he turned and stabbed the leader of the pack in the stomach. Derrick sliced the next closest blood member next to him before he was hit in the back of the head with a hard cover dictionary. Another blood grabbed Derrick from behind and violently, belly to back, slammed him on his head. One of the other Bloods flinched at Butter and he immediately took off running leaving Derrick for dead.

Derrick scrambled back up to his feet as he felt fist coming from all angles. No matter how bad his body was hurting Derrick knew he had to stay on his feet if for whatever reason he hit the floor he knew it was a good chance of him possibly being stomped to death. Derrick dropped his head and swung wildly hoping his fist connected on a few jaws. Just as Derrick was about to get his second wind he felt a sharp knife penetrate his midsection twice before he slowly melted down to the floor. Once Derrick's body hit the floor, all of the Bloods quickly all split up heading in different directions as several C.O.'s came running to Derrick's aide.

Manic
Twenty-Seven

"I want that bitch dead!" Maniac barked as he looked out at the sea of faces in the crowd. He called for an emergency meeting and it seemed like every blood in the city had showed up. "The entire Mason Family is food. I don't care one if you run across their great grandmother!" The bullet wound in his shoulder was driving Maniac crazy. He still couldn't believe that he had allowed Millie to catch him slipping like that. And to think he had actually spared her life. "$50,000 for any member of the Mason Family and $150,000 for Millie Mason. With those kind of numbers involved Maniac knew that the desperate members of the blood organization would be gunning extra hard for the Mason Family. "The Mason Family has too much pride to go into hiding so I'm sure they won't be hard to find," Maniac said with an evil smile on his face. "Time to go hunting."

As all of the Blood members dispersed, Big Blood walked up and hugged Maniac. "You good?"

"I'll be better once bodies of the Mason Family start to drop," Maniac countered. He couldn't remember the last time he was this upset. What really pissed Maniac off was that the streets were now starting to talk. Word on the streets was that

Millie backed her hammer out on Maniac and had him on his knees begging for his life. Maniac knew that the story floating around wasn't authentic but he also knew that the streets would gobble up the story weather fabricated or not. "I want that bitch dead."

Twenty-Eight

Eric sat in his office looking over some paperwork and looking at his laptop both at the same time. Now that the Mason Family was back in business, he found himself busier than ever before. The streets was loving the new product, which meant Eric had to find more ways to clean all the money that was coming in. Eric clicked a few keys on his keyboard when he heard his office phone ring. "Hey, Brittany I don't want to take no calls or see anyone today," he answered.

"I'm sorry to disturb you Eric but there's a detective here to see you," Brittany said waiting for a response.

"Fuck!" Eric mouthed. He wondered what a detective could want to speak to him about. "Send him in." Eric said and then slammed the phone down. Seconds later the door opened and in walked Detective Tyson.

"Good to see you again Eric," Detective Tyson said, extending his hand for a handshake.

Eric looked down at the detective's hand and left him hanging. "How can I help you?"

"Have a few questions I think you can help me with," Detective Tyson said, as his lip curled into a smirk. "Your mansion was burned down last week, you wouldn't happen to know who was responsible for that would you?"

"Nope."

"Have any enemies, Mr. Mason?" Detective Tyson asked. "Anyone that may want you or your loved ones dead?"

"Nope."

"So someone just tried to burn your house down with you and your entire family inside and you don't have a clue who could be responsible for this?"

"Nope."

"Your girlfriend, Nicole Martinez. I pulled her jacket and noticed she's got a rap sheet longer than my dick," Detective Tyson continued. "Anyone you know may want her dead?"

"Nope."

Detective Tyson smiled. "So this is how you want to play this?" he continued. "Cool with me, but just know that I will turn your shitty life upside down and start to look into your little girlfriend's past and see what I dig up. I'm on your ass now!" Detective Tyson barked as he tossed his card down on Eric's desk, turned and headed for the exit.

"Have a nice day!" Eric yelled at the detective's departing back. He knew that the detective sniffing his nose around in the Mason Family's business wouldn't be good for business. Eric pulled out his cell phone and made a quick call.

Brady
Twenty-Nine

Brady sat the table with a huge smile on his face while his men ran all the money that Millie just delivered through several money machines. "I love a woman that knows how to keep her word," Brady handed Millie a glass of wine.

"I don't play when it comes to my money," Millie said as she raised the wine glass up to her lips. "Besides in any relationship you have to be honest, upfront, and you have to be able to keep your word."

Brady grabbed Millie's hand and led her into his sitting room. Before Millie could open her mouth, Brady pressed her back up against the wall and shoved his tongue in her mouth as his hands made their way to her ass. Millie closed her eyes as the peach in between her thighs got soaked instantly. "Wait, I can't do this," Millie huffed as she pushed Brady off of her. "I'm married and this isn't right."

Brady stepped in closer. "Your husband isn't getting out of jail no time soon so stop fooling yourself," Brady slipped his fingers down Millie's pants, felt her wetness, and licked his lips. "I want to taste it!" he said in a strong whisper.

Without warning, Brady lifted Millie up and gently laid her down on the couch. Millie wanted to fight the urge but her body wasn't trying to hear it. Before Millie knew it she was butt naked on the couch with her legs pinned back to her ears, she glanced down and saw Brady's face in between her legs. It had been over fifteen years since Millie had been touched by a man and as much as she hated to admit it this was just what her body needed.

"Yeeeees!" Millie hissed loudly. She grabbed the back of Brady's head and forced it further into her wetness while grinding her hips at the same time. Millie's orgasm shot through her body like a lightning bolt, she was speaking in tongues as if she had caught the Holy Ghost.

Brady slurped on Millie's wetness as if he had something to prove. Once he felt Millie's body shaking, he aggressively turned her over hiking her ass high up in the air. He entered her walls and the tightness immediately gripped him like a tight glove. "Damn baby," Brady growled as he looked down at his manhood and saw that it was covered with Millie's love juices. Brady spread both of Millie's ass cheeks apart and plowed in and out her as if he was possessed, like he was having an out of body experience, like he was trying to punish Millie. "Arghh!" Brady growled then collapsed on top of Millie.

Murder
Thirty

Murder walked through the mall with some new chick he had just met a few weeks ago. The light skin tenderoni had been complaining about Murder not spending enough time with her, so to keep her on his good side, Murder figured the best way to keep her quiet was to take her to the mall and buy her a few things. The new product that Brady had been supplying the Mason Family with was keeping Murder and the rest of the team extremely busy. As Murder strolled through the mall, he spotted an Italian man who was a part of Frank Russo's organization.

"Can we go in the jewelry store baby?" the tenderoni whined.

Murder dug down in his pocket and handed her a hand full of bills. "Yeah go ahead, I'll be in there in a minute I just need to sit down for a second," Murder faked as if he was exhausted and he took a seat on the small bench. Once the tenderoni disappeared inside the jewelry store Murder hopped up off the bench and proceeded to follow the Italian man. Murder picked up his pace; he slipped his hand down in his pocket, and removed a small knife. Murder walked up on the Italian man from behind and jammed his knife deep into his neck and kept on walking like nothing happened. Murder walked past a garbage can and tossed the knife in the trash and smoothly exited the mall. Once in the parking lot Murder took off in a sprint to his car and never looked back.

The Black Dragon
Thirty-One

The Black Dragon sat staked out across the street from Eric Mason's new mansion. He had watched Eric entire the mansion five hours ago. The Black Dragon was waiting for the perfect time to make his move. On his lap rested a five-seven pistol with a silencer attached to the barrel. Al Greene bumped softly through the speakers as the Black Dragon slipped his hands in a pair of tight fitting leather gloves and flexed his fingers. So far he had counted five arm guards patrolling the mansion. The Black Dragon slipped out the car and jogged with a low hunch towards the front of the mansion. The Black Dragon held his weapon with a steady two-handed grip as he fired a shot that landed right between the eyes of the first guard. The Black Dragon moved like a snake using the darkness to his advantage. He ran up on the next guard from behind and slit his throat from ear to ear then violently tossed his body over in the bushes. The Black Dragon pulled a knife from his belt, picked the locks to the side of the house, and let himself inside. Once in the house the Black Dragon felt something crash over his head with a lot of force and power. The Black Dragon hit the floor hard;

the blow caused his vision to become a little blurry. The guard got on top of the Black Dragon and proceeded to pound his face in. The Black Dragon took the blows well then quickly reversed his positioning. He was now on top of the guard rearranging his face with every blow he delivered. The Black Dragon stood to his feet, jumped in the air and stomped down on the guard's head with both feet like, Bruce Lee. The next guard rounded the corner the Black Dragon snatched a knife from off the knife rack and charged at the guard full speed. Before the guard knew what had happened he had several slices all over his body. The Black Dragon finished him off by jamming the knife in the guard's ear. The Black Dragon got ready to make his way up the stairs when he felt the barrel of a gun being pressed into the back of his skull. The Black Dragon ducked just as the gun went off, he spun around, chopped the guard in the throat, and then swept his from under him. From off his back, the guard tried to kick the Black Dragon. The Black Dragon caught the guard's foot and snapped his ankle. The guard howled to the top of his lung before the Black Dragon covered his mouth with a gloved man and jammed a knife in his neck then gave the handle a deadly twist.

Nicole

Thirty-Two

Nicole stepped out of the shower and shook her head when she saw Eric laid across the bed passed out. She knew her man had been working hard so instead of bothering him she pulled the cover over him. Nicole slipped on a laced pair of sexy boy shorts and matching bra when she heard what sounded like a man screaming. Nicole reached under her pillow and grabbed her .380 with the silencer attached to the barrel. Nicole eased her way down the stairs and spotted a guard lying dead in a pool of his own blood in the middle of the hallway. Nicole held a two-handed grip on her weapon and eased her way through the dimly lit kitchen when she saw movement coming from the corner of her eye. Nicole turned and fired several shots in the direction of the figure dressed in all black then quickly took cover behind the refrigerator and waited for some return fire but when none came, Nicole made her move. Nicole slowly slid from behind the refrigerator and slowly made her way over towards the last place she had seen the figure dressed in all black. Nicole eased her way through the house when a foot came out of nowhere and kicked her gun out of her hand.

The Black Dragon quickly followed up with a lightning fast four-punch combination. Nicole was able to block two of the four punches as she returned a few blows of her own. The Black Dragon grabbed Nicole and forced her back against the wall. Nicole quickly countered with a couple of knees to the assassin's rib cage. The Black Dragon blocked Nicole's knees and threw a series of elbow strikes. Nicole's head snapped back as an upper cut landed flush underneath her chin causing her to stumble. The Black Dragon moved in, faked like he was about to throw a jab then raised his foot and stomped down on Nicole's bare feet with his boots trying to break a few of her toes. He then reached out, grabbed Nicole, and tossed her across the dining room table as if she was a rag doll. Nicole hit the floor hard, grabbed a plate off the floor, and threw it as if it were a Frisbee at the Black Dragon's face. The plate shattered against the Black Dragon's forearm as he used it to block his face. Nicole rushed over to the knife rack but before she could grab one the Black Dragon kicked the rack out of arms reach. Nicole threw a five-punch combination that the Black Dragon blocked with ease then reached out, grabbed Nicole by the throat, and tried to choke the life out of her. Nicole slapped the Black Dragon's hand down from around her neck, grabbed him, and rushed him backwards as the two went crashing through the glass door leading out into the hallway.

***

Eric's eyes snapped open when he the loud sound of glass shattering coming from downstairs. He quickly looked over to his right and noticed that Nicole wasn't in the bed. "Shit!" Eric cursed as he grabbed his 9mm from off the night stand and slowly made his way downstairs to see what was going on. When Eric made it downstairs, he saw Nicole and the Black Dragon trying to kill one another.

The Black Dragon grabbed Nicole, slipped behind her, and locked his arms under her neck just as he was about to apply pressure he heard the sound of a gun being cocked.

"Let her go now!" Eric growled as he held a firm two handed grip on his weapon.

"Baby shoot him!" Nicole begged as blood ran freely from her nose. "Shoot him!"

Eric thought about taking the shot but it was too risky for his liking. If he made a mistake and shot Nicole instead of the Black Dragon, he would never be able to forgive himself. "I said put the gun down now!"

"Fuck you!" the Black Dragon capped back. "Shoot and I'll snap this bitch neck!" he threatened.

"Listen, I didn't give Chico your whereabouts," Eric said. "I would never do that.

"Bullshit!" the Black Dragon yelled. "Me and you were the only two who knew about the hit!"

"I swear on my life I had nothing to do with that, but all this violence has to come to a stop," Eric said trying to reason with the assassin. Eric was in a no win situation he just hoped that the assassin would believe him.

Before the Black Dragon could say another word, he felt the barrel of a gun being pressed into the back of his skull.

"Let her go!" Pistol Pete stood behind the Black Dragon, holding a gun to his head. "Don't make me repeat myself!"

The Black Dragon hesitated before finally releasing his grip on Nicole's neck turning her loose. "You're never going to get away with this."

"I already told you I had nothing to do with what happen with your situation," Eric told him for the tenth time. "Now let's end this once and for all."

"Do what you gotta do!" the Black Dragon spat and closed his eyes preparing for the gun shot that he knew was about to come.

"You're free to go," Eric said surprising everyone in the room. The Black Dragon opened his eyes not believing his ears. Eric walked up to him and extended his hand. "I'm not your enemy and I never gave you up."

The Black Dragon looked down at Eric's hand for a second before shaking it. "Thank you," he said with a grateful look on his face. "For this I shall forever be grateful," the Black Dragon said as he turned and made his exit. Once the Black Dragon was gone, Nicole walked up to Eric looking at him as if he was crazy. "What the hell did you just do?"

"It's not good for business to keep the feud going between us," Eric walked in the kitchen and poured himself a stiff drink.

"So what do we do if he comes back?" Nicole asked with a raised brow.

"If he comes back then we kill him."

"I think you're making a big mistake," Nicole said then stormed upstairs.

"She's right," Pistol Pete said speaking for the first time. "You can't trust a man like the Black Dragon."

"Sometimes you just have to roll the dice," Eric raised his glass to his lips and took a deep swig.

Jimmy Mason
Thirty-Three

Jimmy stood in the stash house with an impatient look on his face, he had been standing around waiting for the past fifteen minutes when finally the head runner in the house returned from the back and handed him a duffle bag. "About fucking time!" He snatched the bag from the man's hands and exited the apartment. Jimmy had been working overtime ever since Brady had been supplying them with product. Jimmy tossed the duffle bag in the trunk with the rest of the duffle bags. This was the third stash house he had picked up money from tonight and still had two more to go before he could call it a night. Jimmy pulled away from the curb with a frown on his face he was still pissed off about the beating that he and Cherokee took. Jimmy had several of his men out looking for any member from Frank Russo's family or organization. Jimmy pulled up to the red light and grabbed his cell phone to see if he had received a text message from Murder or anyone else from his crew when a black van pulled up on the side of him and opened fire on his car. Jimmy ducked down and stomped on the gas pedal as a bullet ripped through his shoulder and glass rained down on his head. Jimmy zoomed from lane to lane with a nervous look on his face. He peeked through the rear view mirror and saw a man in an all red hoody hanging halfway out the window with a machine gun in his hand. Jimmy ran through another red light and avoided a collision by a few inches. He quickly clicked on his seat belt and jerked the steering wheel hard to the left causing his body to jerk over towards the passenger seat. Jimmy tried his best to lose the van but it was a task easier said than done. "Shit!" Jimmy cursed as a down pour of rain seemed to come out of nowhere. Jimmy made a sharp right turn when a series of bullets ripped through his trunk and back windshield. One of the bullets managed hit Jimmy's back tire causing him to lose control of the vehicle. Jimmy held on to the steering wheel tightly as the car left the road and entered the woods. Jimmy's car bounced off rocks and trees before finally flipping upside down a couple of times.

The van stopped and four Blood members wearing red hoodies exited the van and made their way down into the woods to finish Jimmy off. Each man wanting to collect the bounty that Maniac placed on the head of any member of the Mason Family. The four Blood members walked up and opened fire on Jimmy's car. One of the Bloods then walked up to the car and snatched the door open only to find it empty. "It's empty," the blood said with a dumbfounded look on his face. Seconds later, a bullet ripped through his chest dropping him right where he stood. The rest of the Bloods quickly ran for cover when they saw their partner drop to the ground.

Jimmy took off in the woods after he shot the first gun man. He knew that would buy him enough time to make a run for it. Seconds later, Jimmy had disappeared through the woods.

Millie Mason
Thirty-Four

Millie stepped foot in the basement of a property that the Mason Family owned looking like a million bucks. She wore an expensive navy blue suit with a pair of navy blue pumps to match. Millie was still floating on clouds from her visit with Brady. She wasn't expecting to take things that far with Brady but it was something about him that she just couldn't resist. Now all Millie had to do was make sure that Derrick didn't find out and keep the money rolling in. Millie entered the room in the basement and saw two men tied down to a chair. "What do we have here?" Millie asked looking over at Jimmy and Murder, whose wife beaters were covered in blood.

"Bloods put a hit out on the Mason Family now I'm going to kill every last one of them one by one," Jimmy turned and punched one of the men tired down to the chair in his mouth knocking out one of his teeth.

Millie removed her suit jacket and handed it to Knuckles. "I had a little run in with one of the head members of the blood organization," Millie informed Jimmy. "Some loser named Maniac."

"So what's the plan?" Jimmy asked.

"If these fuckers want a war then we going to give them one," Millie as she grabbed a hammer out of an old tool box that sat on the shelf. Without warned Millie raised the hammer high over her head and brought it down with great force until it connected with the man's skull. She hit him with the hammer repeatedly until the blood member's brains hung out the side of his head. "Made me mess up my suit," Millie huffed breathing heavily. She knew that this war between the Mason Family and the Bloods was going to get ugly the only problem for the Mason Family was they were outnumbered times four. There was an army of Bloods out hunting members of the Mason Family as if it was a sport.

"A few of those blood clowns tried to run up on me the other but I gave them the shakes," Jimmy said. "Heard some cat named Maniac put a bounty out on our family."

"It ain't the first and it damn sure won't be the last bounty put out on us," Millie said strongly. "It's all a part of the game now; what we have to do is make sure we hit them before they hit us and since it's more of them than us we going to have to take out groups at a time," Millie said looking at everyone in the room.

"With all this banging going on its sure to draw the attention of the police," Murder pointed out. "We might need to rethink this."

"These Bloods are coming to blow your brains out!" Millie snapped. "How you going to think with no brains?" With that being said, Millie and Knuckles turned and made their exit. Millie sat in the back seat of the truck and just stared out the window. She had a lot on her plate right now and just needed a moment to regroup.

"You alright back there?" Knuckles asked in a slow drawl.

"Yeah I'm fine, Knuckles, just drive,"

"I won't let anyone blow your brains out," Knuckles said. "They'll have to blow mines out first."

"I know, Knuckles," Millie smiled. She loved Knuckles and made it her responsibility to always look after him. Millie closed her to take a nap when she felt her cell phone vibrating. Millie grabbed her phone and placed it against her ear. "Hello?"

"Millie what the fuck is going on?" Derrick barked into the phone. His body was still sore from the beating he took the other day.

"Oh hey Derrick," Millie sat straight up. "I been waiting for you to call me."

"Hey Derrick my ass!" Derrick spat. "I was almost killed in here the other day by some young gang members."

"Yeah me and some blood asshole couldn't see eye to eye so we at war," Millie said as if it was no big deal. She knew Derrick was going to be pissed but to be honest she really didn't care.

"You can't just go to war with everyone you have a disagreement with!" Derrick barked. "Cause not only do you put yourself in danger but you also put the family in danger!"

"The last time I checked this family was tough," Millie countered.

"I'm in here with no backup! Derrick, how the hell am I supposed to keep these animals off my ass?"

"You'll figure it out," Millie said in an uninterested tone. Right now, she wasn't in the mood to hear Derrick's mouth; she had a whole lot of better things she could be doing with her time.

"Word?" Derrick said not able to hide the hurt in his voice. In all the years that they had been married Millie had never spoke to him like that. "That's how you talk to me now?"

"Listen Derrick, I ain't about to be sitting on the phone arguing with you all..." Before Millie could even finish her sentence, Derrick had already hung up on her.

$\mathcal{E}ric\ \mathcal{M}ason$

Thirty-Five

Eric sat in the seat of his Range Rover listening to Nicole talk about how she had a plan to get rid of a lot of Blood members at one time. "So you think that could work?" Eric asked.

"Yes I heard they are supposed to be having a big meeting this Friday," Nicole explained. "I say I swing by and take out as many of them as I can."

"I don't know that sounds kind of risky," Eric admitted. He wasn't too fond of sending his fiancé out on such dangerous missions. "What happens if you get spotted, then what?"

"Spotted?" Nicole chuckled. "Baby, I'll be fifty feet away; they won't what's happening to them until it's too late."

"I don't know," the thought of losing Nicole really didn't sit well with Eric. If anything were to happen to her he had no clue what he would do. Nicole grabbed Eric's hand. "Baby you have to trust me," she leaned over and kissed him on the lips. "I can't just sit around and let these "Bloods"…" she made air quotes with her fingers, "tear down our family,

"Baby that's what we paid goons and soldiers for," Eric said. "We only get our hands dirty when we don't have no choice."

"Hey looks like we got company," Pistol Pete said interrupting the two's conversation.

Eric quickly removed his 9mm from his holster. "Bloods or Italians?" he asked. The Mason Family had problems with so many different crews it was beginning to get difficult to keep up.

"Cops," Pistol Pete said over his shoulder as he slowly pulled over to the side of the road. Eric and Nicole quickly tossed their weapons in the stash box and played cool.

Detective Tyson stepped out of his car and slowly walked up to the driver's side of the freshly waxed Range Rover. He pulled out his flash light and shined it Pistol Pete's face. "License and registrations?"

"What did I do?" Pistol Pete asked.

"I'm not going to ask you again," Detective Tyson said in a serious tone. Pistol Pete realized he was in a no win situation and decided to just give the detective his ID. Detective Tyson took the ID and headed back to his car.

"I'm calling Mr. Goldberg first thing in the morning, this is harassment," Eric fumed. "That same detective has been sticking his nose in my business for the past two weeks."

"Just stay cool baby," Nicole coached. She knew they were clean so they had nothing to worry about. If the detective wanted to waste their time then so be it.

"Aw shit!" Eric cursed when he noticed two more patrol cars pull up to the scene. Detective Tyson made his way back to the Range Rover only this time he held his 9mm in his hand.

"Put your hands up and step out of the vehicle slowly!" Detective Tyson yelled with his gun aimed at Pistol Pete's head while the other uniform officers held Eric and Nicole at gunpoint. Pistol Pete slowly stepped out of the truck then was roughly tossed down to the wet ground. Once Pistol Pete was handcuffed, Detective Tyson walked over towards the back door and snatched the door open. "Slowly!" He yelled. "Out of the vehicle!" Once Nicole was out of the truck she too was roughly tossed down to the ground as if she was a piece of trash. Detective Tyson pressed his knee in the middle of Nicole's back and put the cuffs on Nicole's wrist as tight as they could go. He then made his way over to Eric. "Out of the truck tough guy!" Detective Tyson barked as he violently tossed Eric to the ground.

"We didn't even do shit!" Eric winced as the handcuffs pinched his wrist.

"I got a tip on a shooting that just took place and they said that the perps took off in nice shiny Range Rover kind of like this one," Detective Tyson huffed as he watched the uniform officers search the Range Rover.

"This is harassment," Eric spoke in a calm tone. "You'll be hearing from my lawyer."

"Fuck you and your lawyer," Detective Tyson said with a smirk on his face.

"It's clean," one of the uniform officer announced.

"Uncuff these scumbags!" Detective Tyson ordered as he headed back to his car and pulled off.

Nicole rubbed her wrist with a mean look on her face. She had never been violated like this before ever in her life. "I'm going to kill that motherfucker!"

Manic
—
Thirty-Six

M
aniac sat on the bench in the middle of the projects sipping on a cup of Hennessy while he watched his workers make a killing. Maniac no longer lived in the projects but for as much as he stayed in the projects one would never know that. Maniac sipped his Henny as he listened to Big Blood explain why they were losing so many soldiers due to the hands of the Mason Family.

"It's like they have an inside scoop on how to find our peoples," Big Blood said.

"The Mason Family ain't survive this long in the game by being fools," Maniac pointed out. "It may be time for us to call a truce." Maniac's pockets had been taking a hit ever since the war between the Bloods and the Mason Family began. "All these shootings and killing is bringing too many cops around," he explained to Big Blood. "We supposed to be out here getting money not getting arrested."

"But how you think the streets are going to take this when they hear we the ones who called the truce?" Big Blood asked.

Maniac shrugged. "I don't got time to think about nonsense like that. Chico called me last night and he wants to meet with me," Maniac said. "I'm a week late with his payment and it's because of all this heat that this war is causing."

"Damn do we at least have most of his money yet?" Big Blood asked with a raised brow.

"We got about half," Maniac answered as he noticed Big Blood drop down to the ground. Maniac looked down and saw a small hole sitting in the center of Big Blood's forehead when he looked back up a bullet exploded in his face killing him instantly.

Nicole laid flat on her stomach on a roof a few buildings over and had target practice with several Blood members including Maniac and Big Blood. She looked through her scope and watched as the gang members that were still living scrambled for their worthless lives. Nicole gunned down five more gang members before she packed her up her sniper rifle and headed towards the staircase. Nicole took her time going down the stairs; she was in no rush. To be honest Nicole was a little pissed that there weren't more members of the gang present usually on a day like this the projects would be crawling with activity. Nicole stepped out the building and slid in the passenger seat of the awaiting Benz.

"How did it go?" Eric pulled away from the curb. He was eager to hear how everything played out.

"Maniac is dead," Nicole said nonchalantly. "Him and about ten of his buddies," she bragged.

"Damn eleven dead and I didn't even hear one gunshot," Eric pointed out with an amazed looked on his face. He still wasn't too comfortable with his fiancé going out doing all the dirty work but he was now beginning to realize that Nicole was the real deal.

"Didn't I tell you I was good," Nicole smiled.

Eric leaned over and kissed her on the lips. "Nah baby you are the best!"

***

When the couple made it back to their lavish home, their mood quickly went from happy to pissed when they saw Detective Tyson standing out front.

"What the hell do you want now?" Eric growled. He was seriously thinking about putting hands on the punk ass detective and just doing the time but Nicole quickly placed a calming hand on Eric's shoulder to try and help him calm down.

"I need to take your girlfriend down to the stations for a few questions," Detective Tyson said with a smirk on his face.

"Fuck you she ain't going nowhere with you," Eric snapped.

Detective Tyson pulled out a warrant from his inside pocket and held it up to Eric's face. The detective smiled as he grabbed Nicole by the arm and escorted her towards his unmarked car, he then roughly shoved her in the back seat and slammed the door.

"What the hell is all of this about?" Eric yelled as he watched Detective Tyson get behind the wheel and pull off recklessly. Eric immediately pulled out his cell phone and called Mr. Goldberg. Mr. Goldberg was the family lawyer and the best in town and if anyone could get Nicole out of a jam, Eric knew it was him.

***

"So is there anything you want to tell me before we get down to the station?" Detective Tyson peeked at Nicole through the rear view mirror.

"Fuck you pig!"

Detective Tyson nodded his head. "Fine have it your way."

A million thoughts ran through Nicole's mind as she sat in the back seat of the unmarked car. She had no idea why the detective wanted to question her and the real question she wanted to know was how in the hell he was able to get a warrant. For a second Nicole thought about killing the detective but quickly cancelled that idea when she remembered that she wasn't under arrest but only being brought in for questioning. Nicole removed a small blade from the small of her back and stashed it down into the cushion of the seat as Detective Tyson pulled into the police station.

Detective Tyson escorted Nicole through the precinct and led her to the interrogation room at the far end of the hall. "Wait in here; I'll be back in a second."

Nicole helped herself to a seat and got comfortable; she wasn't new to this she knew the routine and prepared herself for the long wait that she knew was ahead of her. Nicole kicked her feet up on the table and closed her eyes. Two hours later, Nicole's eyes shot open when she heard the door open then slam shut.

Detective Tyson stepped in the interrogation room with a smirk on his face and slammed a Manila envelope down in front of Nicole. Nicole grabbed the envelope and viewed the contents that was inside. Nicole's face remained cool as she looked at still pictures of the back of her running out of the warehouse where she had rescued Millie a few weeks back. The only thing working in her favor was the fact that the few pictures was of the back of her head. Nicole knew if she hired

Mr. Goldberg, it was a good chance he'd get the case thrown out.

Nicole tossed the pictures down on the table and shook her head. "This is garbage and you know it."

"That's you in those pictures," Detective Tyson stared Nicole down. "All I need you to do is help me put Millie Mason back in jail," he paused. "We know exactly what she's out here doing and if you don't help you'll be going down right along with her and the rest of her family."

"I ain't saying shit else without a lawyer," Nicole shot back. She was sick of the back and forth game that the cops loved to play.

"Let me explain something to you," Detective Tyson stood over Nicole trying to intimidate her. "When we nail Millie she's going to give you up just like that," he snapped his fingers for extra emphasis. "I'm trying to give you a way out."

Nicole chuckled. "A way out, huh?"

"The case we're building against Millie and the Mason Family is so strong it's going to make their heads spin," Detective Tyson said in a matter of fact tone. "I'm giving you the opportunity to save yourself. You see how easy it was to get the warrant to bring you in."

Nicole said nothing and looked at the detective like he had three heads. Everything he said went in one ear and out the other. "Are we about done here?"

Detective Tyson looked down at Nicole with a disgusted look on his face. "I'm going to make sure all of y'all rot in jail! Now get the fuck out of here!"

Nicole walked out of the precinct with a smile on her face.

Eric Mason
—
Thirty-Seven

Eric sat in his office with a stressed out look on his face it had been hours since the detective had taken Nicole down to the precinct. Eric already had his lawyer Mr. Goldberg looking into the situation but he would feel better once he heard from Nicole himself. Eric badly wanted to go down to the precinct and check up on Nicole but had some very important business he needed to tend to in his office. It was going on two weeks since he'd last saw Millie. Eric had been texting and calling her with no answer or response; all he heard she was supposed to be out in Miami handling some important business. Eric sat down to make a phone call when Pistol Pete entered his office.

"Don't mean to disturb you but you have a visitor," Pistol Pete said as he waved the tall Italian man inside the office.

The Italian man nodded at Eric. "Frank Russo sent me here," he said in a calm tone.

Eric stood to his feet. "You got some big balls coming up in here."

"I'm just here to deliver a message," the Italian man said. "Sell Frank Russo his hotel back and all the blood shed stops;

if you choose not to sell it back him he won't be responsible for what happens to you and your family."

Eric took an aggressive step towards the tall mystery Italian man then quickly stopped in mid stride when he saw the Italian man snatch open his coat. Strapped to his chest was a vest were several sticks of dynamite.

"I wouldn't do that if I were you," the Italian man said with a smile. "You have a week to make your decision," he paused. "Next time I come back we all die," the Italian turned on his heels and made his exit.

"Find out who that jackass is," Eric pour himself a shot of vodka and downed it in one gulp. "I want him dead before the night is out." Eric was about to say something else when he heard his cell phone vibrating on his desk. He down at the caller ID and immediately knew exactly who was calling him. "What's up, Pop?" He answered.

"Your mother has officially lost her mind," was the first thing Derrick said. "She turned her back on me after all the shit I've done for her."

"What y'all fighting about now pop?" Eric asked nonchalantly. Derrick and Millie had been having arguments for years so this wasn't nothing new.

"I'm through with and her shit for good this time," Derrick continued his rank. "And I think she's fucking someone else."

"Why you say that?"

"Because she acting real brand new and chicks only get like that when they get new dick," Derrick explained trying to hide the pain in his voice. "I need you to be my ears and eyes out there while I'm in here."

"Nah come on pops I ain't getting in ya'lls business," Eric countered. The last thing he wanted to do was get caught up in the middle of Derrick and Millie's drama. It wouldn't be fair for him to have to pick a side.

"You know if I find out she's with another man I'm going to kill her, right?" Derrick said in a serious tone.

"Wasn't you cheating on Millie while she was in jail too?" Eric said not understanding his father's point.

"That's different," Derrick said quickly. "Woman aren't supposed to be out there doing what men do."

"If you say so," Eric said only half listening. He had way better things to be doing with his time instead of listening to this nonsense and his tone said just that.

"Just be my eyes and ears while I'm in here, okay."

"I got you Pops I gotta run out real quick call me back some time tonight," Eric rushed his father off the phone.

Millie Mason
—
Thirty-Eight

"**O**h my god, yeees!" Millie purred as Brady slid in and out of her wetness at a steady pace. Millie loved how Brady handled all of her thickness and brought the animal out of her. Brady grabbed a handful of Millie's hair and roughly pulled her head back as he had his way with her. Once the intense sex session was over, Millie laid her head across Brady's chest. "You tore this shit up," Millie said stroking Brady's already huge ego.

Brady smiled. "I have to make sure I keep you around."

"Trust and believe I ain't going nowhere," Millie said planting soft wet kisses on Brady's hairy chest. "You are now officially stuck with me."

"Damn," Brady's joke caused him to receive a punch to the arm. "I really enjoy spending time with you," Brady stroked his fingers through Millie's hair. "I want you around more often."

"Then how the hell am I supposed to make money if I'm here with you all day?" Millie asked.

"Your family has made a lot of good investments," Brady smiled. "I've done my homework on your entire family and

I have to say I like the way your system is set up. I would love to have a guy like Eric on my team to invest some of this money for me."

"Yeah Eric is a genius," Millie said praising her favorite son. "I knew he was going to be special since he was a kid."

"How about if you move out here with me and let's do this the right way," Brady threw it out there. He was beginning to fall head over hills for Millie and didn't see the point wasting anymore time.

"But what about my family?" Millie asked. The question totally caught her off-guard.

"Bring your entire family with and we'll get philthy rich together."

"Can I get a little bit of time to think about this?" Millie asked when out of nowhere the two of them heard the sound of a gun being fired downstairs.

"What the fuck?" Brady shot to his feet as he heard several more shots being fired in rapid secession. Brady quickly rushed over to his gun closet when he felt the cold steel from a gun at the back of his head.

"Get your stupid ass over here!" Millie growled as she roughly slammed Brady down to the floor with one hand and kept her gun trained on him with the other. "Move and I'm going to blow your fucking head off do you understand me!?"

"Millie what the hell are you doing?" Brady spat looking back over his shoulder with a confused look on his face.

"Shut the fuck up!" Millie barked then busted Brady over the head with her pistol. Seconds later, Jimmy Murder and several other goons entered the bedroom and tied Brady up. "Search the place he has tons of cash in here," Millie ordered as she got dress right in front of everyone.

"You and your whole family will be dead in twenty-four hours," Brady said in a calm tone. Without warning, Jimmy raised his leg and stomped Brady's head down into the floor.

Millie reached in a dresser draw and removed a pair of keys. "These keys go to a small single family home that's filled with Brady's entire product," Millie handed Jimmy the keys with a smile on her face. "I'll text you the address."

"Bitch you're never going to get away with this!" Brady struggled to free his hands but it was no use. Millie stood over Brady with her gun aimed at his face.

"I already have," Millie said then pulled the trigger and shot Brady in the face close range. Millie stuck her gun down in her purse while the rest of the goons splashed gasoline all over the beautiful mansion. Jimmy and Murder walked throughout the mansion taking down all of the surveillance cameras. They knew on a job like this they couldn't leave any evidence. One mistake could be extremely costly for all of them. Once the mansion began to go up in flames, Millie walked up to Jimmy and kissed him on the cheek. "Thank you so much for coming to bail mommy out. I texted you the address to the single family home where the product is stashed; go make me proud," she said as everyone exited the mansion and all went in separate directions.

Nicole

Thirty-Nine

N icole stepped foot in the bedroom and saw Eric sitting on the bed doing some work on his laptop. She really didn't want to disturb him but she felt it was either now or never. "Baby we need to talk for a second," Nicole sat down on the bed next to him.

"What's wrong baby?" Eric asked with a concerned look on his face.

"It's that stupid detective," Nicole began. "He really has it out for the Mason Family and I know he has something up his sleeve, but I just don't know what."

"Don't waste time worrying about that clown," Eric said waving him off. "What I need you focusing on is our wedding; have you found a venue yet?"

"Yeah I found one but I'm just so nervous," Nicole admitted. Never in a million years would she have thought that she would be getting married. The feeling was still a little unreal to her and she was having a hard time processing it.

"Baby, you have nothing to be nervous about you are going to look beautiful and it's going to be great," Eric grab her hand and he gently kissed the back of it. "Just relax; our wedding day is going to be the best day of your life, I promise you."

"You're always so positive," Eric said as he heard a light knock at his bedroom door. "Come in!" he called out.

Pistol Pete stuck his head in the room. "Hey boss man can I have a word with you for a second?"

"Yeah I'll be out in a minute," Eric said then leaned over and kissed Nicole on the lips. "I'll be right back baby."

Eric stepped out into the hallway, and just from the look on Pistol Pete's face, he could that the news he was about to deliver couldn't have been good. "What's going on?"

"You ain't going to like this," Pistol Pete said as his eyes went from looking at Eric to down to the floor.

"Hit me with it."

"Millie just killed Brady and burned his house down to the ground," Pistol Pete told him.

"Are you fucking kidding me!?" Eric barked. "Why the fuck would she do some dumb shit like that?"

Pistol Pete shrugged. "I don't know I just got off the phone with Jimmy but he was speaking in so many codes I could barely understand what he was saying."

"Why in the hell would Millie do something so stupid like that?" Eric paced back and forth. None of it made any sense to him. Brady had been supplying them with a great quality of and had been doing straight up business to burn a bridge like that was just stupid. "This is going to hurt our business."

"I'm sure Millie has a plan," Pistol Pete said.

"Yeah to get us all killed!" Eric huffed as he paced back and forth for a few seconds to try and clear his mind. It seemed like forever since Millie was released from jail; she had been doing her best to put the family in bad situation after bad situation. "I'm going to have to have a long talk with Millie as soon as she gets back."

Eric went back in the bedroom and poured himself a drink.

"What's wrong baby?" Nicole asked as soon as Eric stepped back in the room.

"Millie just killed Brady," Eric huffed. "I swear I don't have a clue what be going on in her head."

"Well I'm sure she has a plan," Nicole knew there was always a method to Millie's madness.

"It may be time for us to make our exit from this game and start us a family," Eric threw it out there to see what Nicole's response would be.

"I don't know if I'm ready for all that," Nicole said honestly. She had never thought about being someone's mother, she was just learning how to take care of her own self.

"Of course you are baby," Eric pulled Nicole in close. "You are going to be a great wife and an even better mother," he leaned down and kissed her soft lips.

"Thank you for always believing in me baby," Nicole said as she pushed Eric back onto the bed and slowly straddled him. She leaned over and kissed Eric passionately. "Thank you for everything."

Fourty

Jimmy stepped foot in his house and saw Cherokee sitting up in a chair with her arms folded across her chest and an angry look on her face. "Hey baby, what you doing sitting up in the dark?" he said as he cut the light on.

"So this is what we doing now?" Cherokee stood to her foot and brandished a shiny knife from behind her back. "I've been sitting in this house calling you for the past three days!" she snapped with rage.

"Baby, I was extremely busy and my phone died," Jimmy said telling the truth for the first time. Usually all the excuses he told Cherokee were lies.

"So now you trying to play me like I'm a fool?" Cherokee said as she inched her way closer to Jimmy.

"Listen baby why don't you put the knife down so we can talk," Jimmy suggested.

"Nah I'm done talking," Cherokee said in a voice just above a whisper. "Talking to you gets me nowhere."

"Baby put that knife down!" Jimmy raised his voice hoping it would get Cherokee to cooperate but his plan failed miserably. Cherokee continued to come forward she had a crazy look in her eyes.

"You've hurt me for the last time!" Cherokee snarled as she charged Jimmy with the knife in her hand. Jimmy tried to sidestep the blade but Cherokee managed to slice his arm before he could grab her and wrestle her down to the floor. The two struggled and tussled on the floor for control of the sharp blade neither one wanting to be on the receiving end of the blade.

"Stop! Stop!" Jimmy yelled as the two rolled around on the floor. Finally, Jimmy managed to pry the sharp knife from Cherokee's hand. Jimmy tossed the knife across the room then slapped Cherokee across the face. "What the fuck is wrong with you!?"

Cherokee kicked Jimmy in the groin, shot to her feet, and grabbed Jimmy in a headlock. "I'm going to kill you!" she growled as she tried to ram his head into the wall. Jimmy picked Cherokee up and slammed her down on the couch. Jimmy then quickly got on top of her and pinned her arms down so she couldn't hit him anymore. "Stop!" he screamed in her face. "What the hell is wrong with you!?"

"Get off of me right now!" Cherokee yelled. "I'm going to kill you!"

"Baby! Jimmy yelled. "Enough is enough!" After two minutes of holding her down, he finally let Cherokee up. Cherokee sat up and thought about charging Jimmy again but instead she just sat and started crying. Jimmy sat there and watched Cherokee cry and for the first time he felt her pain.

"Baby, I'm sorry," Jimmy sat down next to Cherokee and rubbed her back. "I promise I won't hurt you again."

"You say the same thing every time!" Cherokee cried. "I'm tired of always fighting with you why can't you just love me and only me? Am I not enough for you? Do I not look good enough? Pussy ain't good enough? What is it?"

"Baby, you are all I need," Jimmy pulled her in close and kissed her neck. He promised from that moment forth he would try to give it his all for their relationship. Jimmy picked Cherokee up, carried her upstairs, and laid her down in the bed.

Millie Mason
===

Fourty-One

M illie and Nicole walked down the street; their hands were full of bags. After the job that Millie just pulled off, she needed some retail therapy to help her think and feel better. Knuckles brought up the ladies rear looking out for any signs of trouble.

"Eric is pissed with you right now," Nicole told Millie.

Millie waved the comment off. "He'll get over it; what Eric has to understand is there ain't no friends in this business. He thinks if someone is nice to him or treats him with respect that they won't put a bullet in the back of his head." She shook her head. "I keep telling him this is a tough business and only the strong survive."

Nicole nodded. "We been talking about maybe starting a family."

Millie stopped and looked Nicole up and down. "A family?" she repeated.

"Yes a family."

"Hmmp," Millie huffed. "I've never heard of an assassin starting a family," she said throwing shade.

"Well I was thinking about and besides I'm not going to be an assassin forever," Nicole pointed out.

"You're letting my son change you and it's disgusting," Millie shook her head. "You the best killer I ever met and now out the blue you want to start a family."

"I'm just thinking about the future Millie, what's wrong with that?" Nicole asked. She was confused why Millie didn't seem happy for her or better yet happy for her own son something about that didn't make sense or sit well with Nicole.

"The only thing y'all should be thinking about right now is how to get this money," Millie said rudely. The truth of the matter was Millie knew that if Nicole did decide to start a family she wouldn't be able to use her as a pawn to do most of her dirty work anymore and that was the real problem and reason why Millie was against them starting a family. The only thing was she couldn't just come out and verbalize that.

"Millie I think these two guys in the grey car is following us," Knuckles said speaking for the first time. Millie and Nicole looked back and saw a grey car with dark tinted windows coasting at a low speed on the side of them. Millie leaned forward and squinted her eyes to try and get a better look inside the vehicle but it was no use the tint were way to dark.

"Fuck this!" Millie huffed as she walked up to the driver's door and kicked it. Instantly the grey car sped. "Did you get the plates?"

"Yeah, looks like Miami tags," Nicole said. The first thing that came to her mind was Brady's people coming to get some payback. "Did anyone see you when you did that thing out in Miami?" Nicole asked with a raised brow.

"Not that I know of," Millie shrugged. She didn't want to admit it but the grey car with smoked out tinted windows startled her a little bit. She had no clue who would be following her in broad daylight especially with Miami tags.

"I think it'll be best if we get off the streets for a little and let things cool off," Nicole suggested.

"I ain't letting no grey car scare me off the streets," Millie huffed. "Plus I still got more shopping to do." The trio continued on with their shopping when they noticed the grey car return.

"Hey I think we should go now before things turn ugly out here," Knuckles suggested as he gripped the handle on his .45. His eyes were glued to the grey car. He had a feeling that whoever was in the grey car spun back around for a reason.

Millie waved the grey car off. "If they want to follow us around while we shop they can be my guest," she huffed. "Plus I can tell they don't want no action."

"Let's just go inside the store just to be safe," Knuckles suggested. Just as the words left his lips the grey car pulled off.

Bad News

Fourty-Two

Bad News sat behind the wheel of his car and watched Eric's every move. He was just waiting for the perfect time to strike. After hearing about Lethal Weapon's death, Bad News knew that he was going to kill the entire Mason Family single handedly if it was the last thing he did. Bad News sat and watched as Eric and Pistol Pete enter a nice size rental property. He waited about ten minutes before he stepped out his vehicle and popped the trunk. Bad News grabbed an A.K. 47 out of his gun bag and headed towards the property to avenge his friend's death.

***

Eric and Pistol Pete followed the realtor throughout the property as they evaluated it. Eric loved making investments; it was just something about his moneymaking that excited him. "I like this place."

"Yeah and I'm sure we can get this clown to go down on the price," Pistol Pete whispered as he looked for any signs of mole on the wall. "Hey have you spoken to your mother yet about that Miami thing?"

"Nah not yet," Eric replied. Ever since Millie got back from Miami, she had been avoiding her son. Eric had called and texted her over twenty times with no answer. "I'm going to swing by her crib tomorrow and see what's up with her," Eric said as he jumped when he heard the front door get kicked open followed by the sound of an assault rifle being fire.

***

Bad News walked up to the front door and kicked it open. He squeezed down on the trigger and swayed his arms from side to side as soon as he stepped foot inside the property. Pistol Pete tackled Eric into the kitchen as several holes decorated the wall where the two men stood just seconds ago. Eric pulled his 9mm from his shoulder hostler and positioned himself behind a wall. Once he heard the gunman's bullets slow down, Eric flung his arm around the corner and fired off four loud thunderous shots. Pistol Pete quickly followed up with three shots of his own. Once Pistol Pete fired his shots, Eric darted out of the kitchen and into the room across the hall. Bad News ran and hid behind a wall closer towards the kitchen. "Come out, come out wherever you are!" He sang then opened fire again. Eric quickly dropped down to the floor when he realized that the A.K. bullets were ripping through the wall as if they were made out of wet paper. Pistol Pete looked across the hall and signaled for Eric to jump out the window and flee the scene but Eric wasn't too comfortable with leaving Pistol Pete behind in a gun battle all by himself. So instead, Eric decide to hang around and stay with his bodyguard. Eric flung his arm around the wall and fired off three more shots. The rental property being empty made it harder for anyone to find a hiding spot. Bad News squeezed down the trigger one last time before he turned and exited the property before the cops arrived.

Eric and Pistol Pete waited like three minutes before the moved from their hiding spots and headed for the front door. Eric snatched the door open and saw several cop cars pulling up to screeching halts. "Shit!" Eric cursed him and Pistol Pete made a dash for the back door. Eric busted out the back door and hopped a fence that landed him in the neighbor's yard. Him and Pistol Pete shook hands then headed in opposite directions. Eric ran through the neighbor's yard when he spotted a police K-9 round the corner coming at him full speed. The dog was running so fast that it forced Eric to make a quick decision. The K-9 leaped through the air. Eric raised his gun and shot the K-9 in the face in midair. The dog hit the ground hard, twitched three times then all movement ceased. Before Eric could make another move, he already had four guns trained on him.

"Put the gun down son!" An officer yelled with a strong two handed grip on his weapon. Having no other options Eric dropped his weapon down to the floor and raised his hands in surrender.

Fourty-Three

"Y ou cheating," Jimmy huffed.

"You just mad because you lost," Cherokee said rubbing it in. Jimmy had taken her to an arcade to help cheer her up especially since he knew how much she loved video games. Cherokee had to admit that since that last fight between the two they had been on much better terms and were beginning to learn how to enjoy one another again. "Thank you baby, I really needed to get out of the house," Cherokee leaned in and kissed Jimmy on the lips.

"Anything for you baby," Jimmy smiled. "And don't think cause you gave me a few kisses that I don't want my rematch."

"You ain't tired of losing yet?" Cherokee said as the two made their way over to the Pacman game and started a new game. The two battled it out until they were interrupted by a rude big-breasted chick.

"Oh hey Jimmy I thought that was you," the big-breasted woman spoke with a big smile on her face. "Don't start acting like no stranger," she spread her arms open for a hug.

"Hey, Simone, long time no see," Jimmy said keeping a fair distance between him and the big-breasted woman.

"What you been hiding from me or something?" Simone smiled. "I called you a couple of times but you ain't answer so I figured you couldn't handle another round of all this."

Jimmy let out a fake chuckle. He glanced over at Cherokee and could tell that she was getting more and more pissed off with each passing second. "Hey, Simone this is my girl Cherokee; Cherokee meet, Simone," he introduced the two.

"Hmmp," Simone huffed, as she looked Cherokee up and down with a nasty look. "But anyway what you doing this weekend?" Before Jimmy could even answer, Cherokee had already swung on Simone. Cherokee punched Simone in the face and rushed her back into the pinball machine. Parents grabbed their kids as the two ladies went blow for blow.

"Yo chill!" Jimmy yelled as he and a few members from the arcade's staff did their best to separate the two women. "Baby let her hair go!" Jimmy yelled as he tried to pry Cherokee's hands from Simone's scalp. Cherokee held a death grip on Simone's hair and refused to release it. Cherokee couldn't believe this chick had the audacity to try and flirt with her man right in her face.

"Bitch don't you ever disrespect me like that again!" Cherokee yelled as she delivered one last punch to Simone's forehead before she finally released her hair.

"Come on baby you have to chill," Jimmy said as he tried to iron out Cherokee's shirt with his hand.

"Bitch was out of line!" Cherokee barked. Her whole mood was now messed up and was now back in a negative space. "So how long you been fucking her?"

"Huh?" Jimmy asked. He could already see where this conversation was headed. "Baby let's just go back to having a good night."

"How can I have a good night when you out here cheating on me!?" Cherokee said taking an aggressive step forward.

Jimmy quickly took a step and made sure he was out of arms reach. "Baby I'm not cheating on you I tried to take you out so we can have a good time."

"I'm ready to go home," Cherokee said then headed towards the exit. She was sick and tired of Jimmy's way. She loved him to death but wasn't too sure about continuing the relationship with him. She had a lot to think about.

Detective Tyson
Fourty-Four

Detective Tyson walked through central booking until he reached the cell he was looking for. He smiled when he looked inside the cell and saw Eric laying in the bench with a stressed out look on his face. "Hey pretty boy, you comfortable?"

"Fuck you," Eric snapped. He knew the detective was there just to try and ruffle his feather. "You ain't got nothing better to do than watch me sleep?"

"I'm here to help you," Detective Tyson said with a smile on his face. "Help me take down your mother and you're free to go."

Eric laughed loudly. "You can't be serious."

"I don't know if you truly understand how much trouble you are in so let me explain it to you," Detective Tyson smiled. "You shot a police dog and that's just like shooting a police officer. You're looking at twenty years in prison."

"For shooting a stupid dog?"

"Well that stupid dog happened to be a police officer," Detective Tyson smiled. "Eric I'm here to help."

"I don't want your help," Eric answered quickly. He knew whenever a cop said they wanted to help you that it really meant that they wanted you to help them and that was a game that Eric wasn't about to play.

"Twenty years is a long time Eric, if I was you I would take some time and reconsider," Detective Tyson smile then walked off leaving Eric with a lot to think about.

***

Four hours later, Eric stepped out of the jail and saw Nicole leaning against the hood of her car waiting for him with a big smile on her face. "Hey baby you okay?"

"Nah I'm starving," Eric said as he hugged Nicole tightly and kissed her on the lips. Eric was happy to finally be out of that filthy jail cell and back out on the streets. Eric got in the passenger seat and strapped on his seat belt.

"So what were they saying?" Nicole asked as she pulled out into traffic.

"Trying to scare me, talking about twenty years," Eric shook his head. "Talking about the dog was an officer."

"The dog?" Nicole asked with her face crumbled up. "These motherfuckers will think of some way to put someone in jail."

"Who you telling," Eric shook his head. "Any word from Millie yet?"

"Yeah I saw her the other day and I ain't really like how she was talking," Nicole said. "You may really need to have a talk with her."

"She was talking crazy like that?"

Nicole shrugged. "I don't know what's going on with Millie right now, you just need to talk to her."

Millie Mason

Fourty-Five

Millie sat at her kitchen table in deep thought. In front of her was a bottle of Effen vodka that she had been taking to the head. Millie's mind was all over the place. A sick part of her missed Brady and wondered what they could have become if she lived a normal life, but the other side of her only cared about the money. Knuckles entered the dining room area and helped himself to a seat across from Millie.

"What's wrong? Why do you look so sad?" Knuckles asked.

"My life is all fucked up, that's what's wrong, Knuckles!" Millie turned the bottle up to her lips and took a deep swig. "I got a lot of money but on the inside I'm miserable," a couple of tears rolled down her face.

"I've been saving all the money you've been giving me and I can take you to Disney World if that will make you feel better," Knuckles said innocently. "And we can take a picture with Mickey Mouse."

Knuckle's words brought a smile to Millie's face. "Thanks, Knuckles but I think I'll treat you to Disney World, how does that sound to you?"

"Yeeees!" Knuckles said excitedly, sounding like a big ass kid.

"I love you, Knuckles," Millie walked around the table and gave him a tight hug. "Have you been reading those books I brought for you like you promised you would?"

"No," Knuckles answered hanging his head.

"Why not? I told you have to read that's the only way you going to learn is by reading and building your vocabulary," Millie stressed.

"I know Millie, but those books you gave me had some really big words in them and I didn't know what any of them meant," Knuckles said honestly.

"What kind of big words?"

"Big words like manager and helicopter," Knuckles said seriously.

"It's okay, Knuckles I promise I'm going to help you," Millie rubbed his back as she noticed Eric and Pistol Pete walk through the front door.

"I've been calling you for over a week!" Eric huffed. "What you screening my calls now?"

"Been going through a lot over here," Millie took another long swig from her bottle.

"What the fuck happened with Brady?"

"He had to go," Millie shrugged. "We got over a thousand kilos free of charge. With that type of money we can go buy us an island somewhere and never come back."

"First we have to sell all of it without getting killed or arrested!" Eric snapped. "What happens if Brady's people come back for revenge?"

Millie took a swig from her bottle and gave Eric a look of disgust. "You are such a bitch!"

"What you just said?"

"Man up you sound like a pussy!" Millie said. "What you scared or something?"

"Fuck you Millie!" Eric yelled. "I'm out! All you going to do is get our entire family killed!"

"You always been a pussy since you were a baby," Millie slurred. "Keep your weak ass from around me," she waved him off in a dismissive manner.

Eric looked at his mother one last time then turned and made his exit. Millie's words cut through him like a knife. He couldn't believe the words that came out of her mouth. Eric was always told when someone shows you who they are to believe them. Eric got in the back seat of his Range Rover and waited for Pistol Pete to come out of the house.

Pistol Pete stood in the house looking at Millie. "You was wrong Millie; you didn't have to go that far. Eric is still your son."

"Fuck him I'm tired of carrying that boy. I've been carrying him since he came out of me," Millie huffed and turned her bottle up to her lips again. "It's time for him to stop crying and learn how to be a man. I can't help him no more."

"You're losing yourself," Pistol Pete told her. "And I hope you can catch yourself before it's too late," he said then made his exit.

"Well fuck you too!" Millie yelled at Pistol Pete's departing back. She looked down at her buzzing iPhone, saw Derrick's name flashing across the screen she quickly hit ignore, and slipped her phone back in her pocket.

***

Pistol Pete got back in the Range Rover and pulled back out into traffic. "Sorry about what happened back there."

"It's not your fault," Eric said.

"Don't mind your mother, she was just drunk."

"Nah she said how she really felt about me and it's cool, at least now I know," Eric said trying to hide the hurt that was on his face. On the inside he felt so small and worthless but on the outside he had no choice but to remain strong.

"Millie's a good person but right now she's not acting like the intelligent woman that I met several years ago," Pistol Pete fumed. "Hopefully she'll get her act together."

Derrick Mason

Fourty-Six

D errick Mason walked down the tier with an angry look on his face. The streets were talking about Millie and her crazy antics. The jail was buzzing and the word was Millie was responsible for the death of Brady and a lot of people weren't too happy about that. Now Derrick had a tough decision to make. He continued down the tier until he reached the cell of a Jamaican man with huge muscles. "What's up Bob, you wanted to see me?"

"Sit!" Bob said in a deep voice. "It's been brought to my attention that your wife is responsible for the death of Brady. Brady supplied all of the Jamaican and Haitian people as well as most of the Bloods in the south," Bob paused. "So since we can't get to your wife, you become the next best thing."

"But me and my wife aren't even together anymore," Derrick said but he could tell that the Jamaican man could care less.

"Long story short either you give up the whereabouts of your wife or you take her punishment," Bob said, laying it out in black and white. He wasn't the one for the long unnecessary conversations.

Derrick grabbed a piece of paper off the shelf and scribbled something down then handed it to, Bob. "Here's her address just do me one favor."

"What's that?" Bob asked.

"Make it messy," Derrick said.

Bad News

Fourty-Seven

Bad News sat in the strip club tossing dollars up on the stage. He had his eye on a light skin beauty that he planned to make an offer she wouldn't be able to refuse at the end of the night. Bad News was well over his alcohol limit but he continued to drink anyway. He was still grieving over his friend, Lethal Weapon. The fact that he couldn't be here to enjoy the simple things like having a drink still bothered Bad News. He slapped a dancer on the ass as she walked past. Bad News stood to his feet and slowly half walked and half wobbled over to the back of the strip club and entered the restroom. He walked up to a urinal, threw his head back, and emptied his bladder. When Bad News was done, he heard the bathroom door open, close, and then lock. He spun around and saw Jimmy and Murder standing there with no nonsense looks on their faces

"Aren't you going to wash your hands?" Jimmy asked sarcastically as he pulled a big hunting knife from the small of his back and moved in on Bad News. Bad News raised his hands to defend himself but before he knew what happened he already been sliced five times. Bad News stumbled back into the sink and watched as blood spilled from his body.

"Fuck both of y'all," Bad News flashed a smile as Jimmy walked up and jammed his knife in Bad News stomach repeatedly until the big man collapsed down to the dirty rest room floor and stopped moving. Jimmy brought his leg back and violently kicked Bad News in the face before the two men exited the restroom.

Jimmy Mason
Fourty-Eight

The next day Jimmy sat on the couch in his boxers playing a game of madden on his PS4. The last couple of weeks of his life had been stressful so now he was taking time to relax and unwind.

"Baby you hungry?" A brown skin woman walked out into the living room in the nude with a bright smile on her face.

"Nah I'm good, Olivia," Jimmy said never taking his eyes off the TV screen. Olivia was one of Jimmy's new play things that he was starting to fall hard for.

"Can I play?" Olivia asked playfully, as she rubbed Jimmy's shoulders. Jimmy paused his game and picked Olivia up and her legs quickly clamped around his waist as the kissed like young teenage kids. Jimmy sat Olivia on the counter, dipped low and kicked on the pearl that rested between her legs

"Sssss," Olivia hissed when she felt Jimmy's tongue lapping over her clit. She grabbed the back of Jimmy's head forcing his face further into her wetness. Jimmy moaned loudly as he slurped all over Olivia's wetness.

"I want to feel it!" Olivia growled as she forced Jimmy's pants down, grabbed his pole, and forced it inside of her. "Aww," Olivia moaned, as she looked Jimmy in his eyes as he stroked her to heaven.

Eric Mason

Fourty-Nine

Eric and Nicole laid across the couch eating pizza, watching season two of the web series *The Hand I Was Dealt*. Eric had to admit it felt good being able to sit home and spend time with his fiancé all day. They both shared a bottle of wine. Eric took a swig of wine straight from the bottle then passed the bottle to Nicole. Nicole took a swig from the bottle and smiled. "I love spending time with you."

"Oh really?" Eric said as he leaned over and kissed her on the lips. "You don't miss your job?"

"You know what's so strange? I thought I would but I haven't even thought about nothing work related for the past week," Nicole admitted. Once upon a time, Nicole loved her job but now she felt different as if she was growing into her womanhood and finally growing up. Eric was showing her that they were several ways to make money with selling drugs and killing people and that's what she loved about him and their relationship. In all of Nicole's years living, she had never felt the type of love that Eric was giving her, not even from her parents.

"So have you found a venue for the wedding yet?" Eric asked as he rubbed on Nicole's ass.

"Yes I found a nice spot that I loved and it fits about two hundred people," Nicole said with an excited look on her face. Eric got ready to reply when he heard a strong knock at the front door. Eric stood to his feet as Nicole passed him a gun. Eric walked towards the door with caution; he opened the door and saw Cherokee standing on the other side with a mean look on her face.

"Hey Eric sorry for just popping up at your house like this but have you seen Jimmy?" Cherokee asked.

"Nah, sorry Cherokee, I haven't heard from or seen Jimmy in a couple of days," Eric said as he took in Cherokee's appearance. She wore sneakers and an all-black sweat suit not to mention her hair looked like stir fried shit.

"Well I'm letting you know now that when I find your brother I'm going to kill him," Cherokee said meaning every word. "He hasn't been home in a week and he won't answer any of my calls."

"Damn, I'm sorry to hear that Cherokee," Eric said sincerely. He felt bad to hear how bad his brother was treating Cherokee especially since he knew that she was a good woman.

"I just can't figure out why he's doing this to me," Cherokee said as tears streamed down her cheeks. "I cook, I clean, I fuck, and suck him how he wants I don't know what else to do."

"Come here," Nicole said as she pulled Cherokee in and hugged her tightly. "It's going to be alright," she whispered as she rubbed Cherokee's back.

"I swear to god when I catch him I'm going to kill him and whatever bitch he's with," Cherokee cried. Visions of Jimmy making love to strange women that same way he made love to her filled Cherokee's head. "I heard the last place people saw him was with some brown skin slut over in the Bronx."

Eric walked over. "Listen Cherokee, I'm going to be straight up with you, you need to leave my brother and move on with your life because the only thing that's going to happen is you're just going to keep on getting hurt."

Cherokee stood to her and thanked both Eric and Nicole then headed for the exit. Eric watched Cherokee walk out the front door and knew that when she caught up with Jimmy all hell was going to break loose.

Knuckles
Fifty

K nuckles stood in the Chinese restaurant waiting for his food when he noticed three strong looking Jamaican men enter the restaurant.

"Hey mon, where me find ay Millie?" one of the Jamaican's asked aggressively.

"I'm sorry but I speak English," Knuckles said, not meaning any disrespect.

"Bredrin me no come here to play," the Jamaican said as he brandished a machete. Knuckles looked down at the machete and stole on the Jamaican man knocking him out with one punch. The two other Jamaicans rushed the big man. Knuckles grabbed the first man and delivered a head-butt that shattered the Jamaican's nose, sending blood squirting all over the place. Knuckles then wrapped his big mitts around the man's throat and proceeded to squeeze the life out of him. The Jamaican's man's eyes began to roll in his head when the last Jamaican hit Knuckles across the back with a wooden broomstick. The broom made contact with Knuckles back and snapped in half. Knuckles turned and grabbed the last Jamaican and tossed him through the glass door out onto the streets. Knuckles stepped outside and spotted two more Jamaicans. One held a baseball bat while the cracked a bottle on the cement and used the rigged neck of the bottle as a weapon. The first Jamaican swung the bat with all his might only to watch snap over the big man's forearm. Knuckles grabbed the man by his long dread locks and snapped his neck. Knuckles then walked up to the last Jamaican standing. The Jamaican tried to jam the broken beer bottle in Knuckles stomach but the big man caught the Jamaican's wrist and snapped it forcing him to release the beer bottle and howl in pain. By now a crowd started to form and people held out their smart phones recording everything that took place. A few bystanders even yelled out, "Worldstar!"

Knuckles grabbed the last Jamaican and power bombed him down on the concrete. From how the man landed on his neck chances were that was the last time he would ever open his eyes again. Once his work was done, Knuckles walked off but as he walked he noticed the same gray car following him again. Not knowing what else to do, Knuckles took off in a sprint and turned down a dark street. Knuckles look back behind him and noticed the gray car swerve around the corner at a fast speed.

Knuckles ran as fast as he could then turned around and all he saw were headlights. "Oh shit!" Knuckles cursed as the gray car hit him going sixty miles per hour. Knuckles bounced off the windshield and then up into the air only to violently fall face first down onto the unforgiven concrete. The gray car kept on moving never looking back.

Millie Mason

Fifty-One

When Millie got wind of what had happened to Knuckles she made a beeline straight for the hospital. She vowed to kill whoever was responsible for hurting her good friend Knuckles. Millie stepped foot in the hospital and the first thing she noticed her that there were cops everywhere. Millie walked up to the front door and gave Knuckles information, and in return, she was told what room he was in. Millie stepped off the elevator and power walked down the hall until she reached the room that she was looking for. Millie stepped in the room and saw Knuckles laying in the hospital bed with a cast on his leg and arm along with a few bandages wrapped around his head. "Are you okay?"

Knuckles face lit up when he saw Millie. "Hey Millie, yeah I'm okay."

"What happened?"

"I'm not sure. I went to go and get me some Chinese food when three men walked in the restaurant and tried to attack me," Knuckles told her.

"Do you remember what anyone of them may have looked like?" Millie asked hoping to find out who was behind this ambush.

"No, I never seen them before but they were Jamaican," Knuckles said. "They talked funny."

"They had an accent?" Millie asked.

"No, I didn't have an accident," Knuckles said not understanding.

"Come on, I'm taking you home with me," Millie as she grabbed a wheelchair and rolled it over towards the bed.

"But the doctors said I need to stay here for a few nights," Knuckles said innocently.

"Fuck what the doctors said!" Millie spat. "Now get your ass in this chair so I can take you home." A few nurses had to tell help Knuckles out of the bed and into the wheelchair. Millie rolled Knuckles onto the elevator. "So you said some Jamaican's did this to you right?"

"No I killed all of them," Knuckles said. "When I was on my way home I noticed that same gray car following me so I took off running but the car was faster."

"That same gray car?" Millie asked. Just hearing about the gray car made her upset. What really pissed her off about the gray car was that she had no clue who was inside. Millie rolled Knuckles outside and the first thing Millie saw when she looked up was that same gray car sitting at the end of the parking lot. A few of Millie's bodyguards helped Knuckles out of the wheel chair and onto the back of a pickup truck.

"I'll be right back," Millie said as she headed in the direction of the gray car. She reached down in her purse and removed her .380 and attached a silencer to the barrel. "You motherfuckers wanna play?" she said to herself. As soon as Millie got within striking distance of the gray car, it abruptly pulled out of the parking lot like a bat out of hell. "That's what the fuck I thought!" she yelled at the car's tail lights.

Jimmy Mason

Fifty-Two

Jimmy sat in the hookah lounge with Olivia on his lap as the two enjoyed some watermelon-flavored hookah. "You looking good enough to eat right now," Jimmy said as he nibbled on the nape of Olivia's neck.

"Don't start something that you know you can't finish," Olivia teased as she discreetly fondled Jimmy's pole. Jimmy bobbed his head to music that bumped through the speakers. Spending time with Olivia was like a breath of fresh air. With her, he didn't have to worry about arguing or fighting about every little thing not to mention she was just all around the board cool.

Olivia leaned down and kissed Jimmy on the lips. "What you over there thinking about?"

"Taking you in the bathroom, bending you over the sink, and letting you have it," Jimmy said with his teeth gritted together.

"You keep talking like that and you going to make me fall in love with you," Olivia said as a Hennessy bottle bounced off the side of her head.

"What the fuck?" Jimmy said as he looked up and saw Cherokee standing over Olivia bashing her face in with the Hennessy bottle. Jimmy tackled Cherokee down to the floor just to restrain her and stop her from catching a body. "Yo chill out!" Jimmy yelled as Cherokee bit down into his arm forcing him to release his grip on her. Cherokee shot to her feet and attacked Jimmy like a wild animal. She punched Jimmy in his face several times, bit him, ripped his shirt, and tried to rake his eyes out before security came to Jimmy's rescue and roughly escorted Cherokee out of the club. Jimmy walked over and saw a crowd of people standing over Olivia's body. There was blood everywhere but on a good note, Jimmy could see Olivia's chest and stomach rising and sinking with each breath she took. "Thank god she's still alive," Jimmy thought as he went to the bathroom to look over his appearance. From the stinging in his face he could tell that the scratches on his face were pretty deep. Jimmy looked in the mirror and was happy to find out that the damage wasn't as bad as he thought it would be. As Jimmy was looking over his wounds, he heard the bathroom door open and in stepped a scrawny looking man with glasses.

"Hey man, I saw what happened back there," the scrawny man said. "And I think you owe both of those ladies an apology."

Jimmy walked right up to the scrawny man and smacked the shit out of him sending his glasses flying across the bathroom. He then followed up by picking the scrawny man up and dumping him down on his head. "How bout that!" Jimmy cleared his throat and spat on the scrawny man before making his exit.

Fifty-Three

Frank Russo sat at a five-star steakhouse enjoying a nice meal over in a private section in the back. Today he was in a very good mood because when he woke up today he had received a phone call from Eric Mason asking to meet so they could discuss the possibility of him selling the hotel back to Frank. Frank enjoyed his meal with four of his best bodyguards just in case Eric had something tricky up his sleeve. Eric entered the restaurant hand in hand with Nicole. They were both dressed to impress.

"Thank you for taking this time to meet me," Eric shook Frank's hand. "This is my fiancé Nicole.

"You are beautiful," Frank said as he kissed the back of Nicole's hand and openly checked her out.

"So I'm here to let you know that I was thinking about buying the rest of your hotels from you," Eric said, as he poured himself a glass of red wine.

"What is this some kind of fucking joke?" Frank said. His tone had rose to the next level. "I hope you didn't come here to waste my time!"

"Of course not," Eric sipped his wine. "I'm willing to make you a hell of an offer."

Frank Russo leaned back and hog spit in Eric's face. "You stupid nigger, I told you not to waste my fucking time." Without warning, Nicole spit a blade out of her mouth, jumped up, and slit the throat of the guard that stood nearest to her. The next guard went to make a move and grab Nicole, but he quickly pulled his arm back when he felt the sting of the blade slide across his arm. The next guard threw a punch at Nicole's face. She easily weaved the punch and landed three of her own dropping the big man right where he stood. The last guard roughly grabbed Nicole from behind and she used his momentum against him, spun him around, snatched the wine bottle off the table, and cracked it over his head. Nicole then walked over to the guard whose arm she cut and slit his throat from ear to ear leaving him on the floor to gargle on his own blood.

Eric smiled as he wiped the saliva from his face with a napkin. "Now like I was saying, I'm going to make you a nice offer for the rest of your hotels."

Frank sat at the table with a scared and nervous look on his face. "Eric please, what you're doing isn't right."

Eric pulled a contract out of a Manila envelope and slid it across the table to Frank. "I think you know what to do."

"My family has owned these hotels and have passed them on for generations," Frank said looking for sympathy.

"That ain't got nothing to do with me," Eric said coldly. "Either sign this contract with ink or I'll do it with your blood."

Not having too much of a choice Frank pulled out a pen, signed the contract, and then slid it back over to Eric. "You're never going to get away with this!"

"I just did," Eric said as he watched Nicole get up and slice Frank Russo's throat.

Fifty-Four

"**W**ord, all that happened that the hookah lounge?" Murder asked mad he had missed out on some good action. It may have been a good thing that Murder wasn't at the hookah lounge that night because if he were more than likely someone would have lost their life that night. "So have you spoke to Cherokee since that night?"

"Nope," Jimmy answered. "I tried to call her a few times but she won't pick up for my number." Jimmy knew Cherokee was still mad at him and probably wouldn't be speaking to him for a while so he decided to just give her some space so she could heal and recover.

"With the way all this work is moving I may be able to retire within six months," Murder joked. He loved working with the Mason Family because they treated him like family instead of a business associate.

"I ain't never going to retire," Jimmy huffed. "I'm going to get money until the day I die."

"But fuck all that, what's up with these clowns in this gray car that keeps on following your mother around? Any word on them yet?

"Nah not yet, we still looking into that but as soon as I hear something you know you'll be the first to know," Jimmy said as he noticed three rough-faced men headed in him and Murder's direction.

"Yo which one you clown ass niggaz is Jimmy?" The man with the biggest muscles out the group spoke in an intimidating tone.

"Yo my man I'm going to tell you this one time and one time only," Jimmy spoke in a calm tone. "You don't want these kind of problem so I'm going to give you a pass and let you leave now."

"Listen I'm Olivia's brother and for the past few weeks all she could seem to talk about was you and now that she's been in the hospital. I want to know why the fuck you ain't been to visit her yet," Olivia's brother bark. "Especially since you're the reason she's in the hospital to begin with,"

"I been busy that's why I haven't been to see her," Jimmy said nonchalantly. He made it seem like he could less about Olivia and the condition she was in.

"You been busy huh?" Olivia's brother looked around. "Don't look like you that busy to me you sitting over here talking to your man."

Murder listened to all this nonsense for as long as he could before he turned and swung on Olivia's brother punching him in the mouth. From there all hell broke loose. Jimmy fought both of Olivia's brother friends both at the same time while Murder easily handled Olivia's brother. Murder tapped Olivia's brother pockets after he beat him unconscious. Murder then pulled his 9mm from his waistband and shot both of the other two men in the leg. Before him and Jimmy hopped in their Benz and fled the scene.

Fifty-Five

Millie sat inside a Denny's sipping on some tea. She was waiting to meet up with some young cat that was moving a lot of weight out in Staten Island. That was a market that Millie hadn't stepped into yet and figure now would be a great time to get that ball rolling. The guy she was supposed to be meeting was some young cat that went by the name, Young Fly. Millie didn't really care for the name but figured she'd sit down and hear him out. But before Young Fly could show up three ugly Jamaican men stormed in the Denny's with guns in their hands. Millie hand came out of her purse quickness as she dropped the first gunman with a shot to the chest. Millie dashed out of her seat as a bullet grazed the side of her head taking off a strip of her hair in the process. Millie dashed back into the kitchen area and took cover behind a big metal looking refrigerator. The first Jamaican ran wildly around the corner and into the kitchen area and was rewarded with a bullet to the throat. Millie stepped over the dead man's body as she slowly searched for the last gunman. Millie peeked her head around the corner and saw the final gunman run out of the restaurant. That may have been the smartest decision he made in his entire life. Millie quickly headed for the exit when she looked up and looked directly into the camera that rested on the wall directly above the door. "Shit!" she cursed as she continued on out of the restaurant.

***

"Fuck! Fuck! Fuck!" Millie cursed as she flew down the highway. She knew it would only be a matter of time before the cops were on her ass. But she figured she had time to go back to the house, grab her money, some clothes, Knuckles, and then disappear forever. Millie pulled out her cellphone and called Jimmy. "Hey I need you to meet me at my house in twenty minutes, it's an emergency! Twenty minutes!" she yelled then ended the call. Millie zoomed from lane to lane going ninety miles per hour she knew time was against her so she had to move fast. Millie pulled into her drive way and stomped on the brakes causing her Benz to skid. Millie hopped out car and rushed towards the front of her house. She was moving so fast that she never noticed the gray car sitting across the street.

Millie came busting through her front door and stopped in mid-stride. In the living room sat Knuckles tied down to a chair with a strip of duct tape covering his mouth. Standing over Knuckles were two big men who looked like NFL linebackers. And over on the couch to Millie's right sat Slim. He was Brady's right-hand man and head of his security. He sat in an expensive suit with his legs crossed. "So glad you could finally join us," Slim said with a neutral look on his. Immediately, one of the linebackers frisked Millie and removed all of her weapons.

"What's this all about, Slim?" Millie said pretending like she had no clue on what was going on.

"I think we both know why I'm here," Slim stood to his feet and removed a gun from his shoulder holster. He walked up to Knuckles and shot him in the foot. "POW!"

Knuckles let out a loud drawn-out muffle from behind the tape that covered his mouth. Millie tried to attack Slim but was quickly tackled down to the floor and restrained.

"You trying to say something you fucking retard?" Slim taunted as he turned back slapped Knuckles across the face with his gun. "I'm surprised you're still alive especially after the way I hit you with my gray car the other day," Slim smiled. "But no need to worry, I promise I'll finish the job today. But first I have to make you suffer," Slim smiled as he walked over to his duffle bag that laid on the floor and removed a power drill.

"Listen Slim, please don't do this," Millie begged. "Whatever I did wrong I promise I can fix it."

"I think it's a little too late for that," Slim hit the power button on the drill and made it come to life. Knuckles eyes got as big as fifty-cent pieces when he saw Slim aim the drill down at his kneecap.

"Mmm... hmm... mm... bmm" Knuckles moaned from behind the tape. Slim ignored the big man cries for help and slowly pressed the drill down into his knee cap.

"Mmmmmmmmm!" Knuckles cried from behind the tape.

"That's enough!" Millie cried as she was forced to watch, Knuckles get tortured. She felt so bad that all of this was happening to Knuckles because of her. "Let him go and torture me please," Millie begged as she struggled to free herself

"Now let's do the other knee shall we?" Slim said with a sickening smile on his face. He slowly pushed the drill down into Knuckles kneecap and held it there for a second. "That feel good?" He taunted the big man.

Tears ran freely down Millie's face. To see how much pain Knuckles was in broke her heart into pieces. If Millie could have traded her life for Knuckles, she would have jumped on it in a split second. But unfortunately she was being forced to watch a longtime friend of hers get tortured to death.

Slim cut the power drill off, sat it on the table, then walked back over to his bag and removed an electrical saw.

"Slim please he's already suffered enough, let him go and take me instead he ain't got nothing to do with this shit anyway," Millie pleaded hoping she could somehow save Knuckles life.

Slim ignored all of Millie's pleas and proceeded to saw Knuckles legs off. Slim went from leg to leg then began working his way upwards.

"I'm so sorry, Knuckles," Millie cried her head off as she laid on the floor looking at Knuckles lifeless body lying on the floor in a bunch of pieces.

Slim kneeled down in front of Millie's his face was covered in blood but yet you could still see his bright smile. "Where would you like to start?" he asked. "Upper body of lower body?"

"Fuck you!" Millie spat. If looks could kill Slim would have been dead a long time ago. In all honesty, Millie was ready to get this over with. If she was about to die she wasn't about to give her enemies the satisfaction of hearing her scream. Millie was ready to go out like a soldier so her name could definitely go down in the history books as one of the best to ever do it.

Slim grabbed the power saw and stood over Millie, but before he could do anything hurtful to her, an infrared beam landed right in between his eyes. A second later, Slim's brains were all over the hard wood floors. Next, each one of Slim's guards dropped face first one after another.

Millie slowly picked herself up off the floor, looked over at what was left of Knuckles, and let out a heartfelt cry. It was all her fault why he had lost his life. What bothered Millie the most was that Knuckles had died before she had a chance to make his dream come true and take him to Disney World. "I'm sorry, Knuckles!"

A few seconds later, Jimmy came through the door like a mad man. "You alright?" he asked as he examined his mother to make sure she was okay.

"That was good shooting back there son," Millie patted Jimmy on the back. Millie was thankful for Jimmy because if he didn't show up when he did Millie was sure that she'd be laying somewhere on that floor right next to Knuckles.

"Thank me later, right now we have to go!" Jimmy said as he could hear the sirens getting louder and louder with each passing second.

Millie walked over to her gun closet and pulled out an M-16 assault rifle that she never took out the house and planned to only use if totally necessary and today seemed and felt like one of those days. "You can go without me cause I'm staying," Millie said meaning every word that came out of her mouth.

"Huh?" Jimmy echoed. Her words had caught him off guard and didn't quite register at the moment. "I'm serious we have to go now!!"

"You go son, I'm staying," Millie flashed a smile. She was sick and tired of running and today was the day that she planned to stop running forever. "I'm at peace with my decision son," Millie leaned in and hugged Jimmy tightly damn near squeezing the life out of him. "You make sure you tell Eric I love him and I didn't mean those hurtful things that I said to him. Take care of your brother Jimmy I love you but you have to go!" She shoved him towards the door.

"But Eric is getting married today," Jimmy reminded his mother hoping that would get her to change her mind and leave with him.

"I'll have to make it up to him! Now Go!" Millie yelled. Once Jimmy was gone, Millie sat on the couch with her M-16 laying across her lap. "Come on you motherfuckers."

Fifty-Six

J immy sat in his car a block away from Millie's house. He watched as almost twenty cop cars surrounded her and drawn their weapons. "Fuck!" Jimmy cursed loudly. Seeing all the police surround his mother's house made Jimmy wish he had just carried her out the house whether she liked it or not even if Millie would have been kicking and screaming she would of still been alive to talk about it. Tears rolled down Jimmy's face as he watched several officers bust through the front door. Within seconds, all that could heard was the sound of loud gunfire coming from what sounded like about twenty different guns. Jimmy wiped his eyes as he pulled away from the curb feeling like he had just lost a piece of himself.

***

Millie stood up from the couch when she heard footsteps scattering around the door. She positioned herself behind a wall and kept her assault rifle trained on the front door. Millie held her gun trained at the door for about two minutes before the door was finally kicked open. Millie's assault rifle rattled in her hand as the first five cops that ran through the front door went down hard and fast. The cops then began shooting through the window giving cover to the next batch of cops that enter the gun fight through the front door. Millie held her up until a gang of cops kicked down the back door. A bullet hit Millie in the breast taking her down to the floor. She looked up at the ceiling and smiled as she saw all the cops standing over her. Millie reached in her waistband and pulled out her .380 but before she got a chance to use it the police fired over fifty rounds into Millie's body silencing her forever.

Fifty-Seven

Eric stood in the back as Pistol Pete fixed his tie for him. Eric knew he wanted to spend the rest of his life with Nicole but for some reason today, he was extremely nervous. He didn't know if it was because he was about to get married or because Millie nor Jimmy had showed up yet. "Heard anything from Millie?"

Pistol Pete shook his head no. He had been trying to call Millie for the past three hours but her phone kept going straight to voicemail. "Don't worry about them, they'll be here. You just focus on marrying that beautiful bride of yours. Today is your day."

The pastor knocked on the door and stuck his head in. "Waiting on you," he said in a friendly tone.

"I'll be out in five minutes," Eric said politely. He was trying to wait till the last minute to give Millie and Jimmy a chance to show up but he couldn't wait any longer the show had to go on with or without them.

"Let's do this," Pistol Pete smiled as he hugged Eric and patted him on the back. Eric, Pistol Pete, and the rest of the groomsmen walked out and took their positions. Eric look at the sea of faces in attendance and couldn't believe this was really happening. Eric Mason was about to give the woman he called his best friend his last name. Two minutes later, Nicole's bridesmaids came out looking beautiful. The longer Eric stood up there next to the pastor the more nervous he was becoming. It felt like his stomach was on a rollercoaster. A few seconds later, Nicole made her way around the corner and down the aisle. She wore a beautiful white dress that dragged lightly across the floor. Everyone in attendance pulled out their smart phones and camera and began snapping pictures trying to capture every moment of this beautiful day. A big smile crept up on Eric's face when he saw Nicole in her wedding dress. Nicole's face was beautifully done by a makeup artist and even though you couldn't see her shoes, they were beautiful just like the rest of her. Nicole finally made it down the aisle and stood face to face with Eric. The two were like two high school kids that couldn't stop smiling at one another.

"Do you mind holding her hand?" Pastor asked as he opened his. Just as he was about to get the ceremony started a loud bang erupted from the front of the church causing everyone to look towards the entrance.

Detective Tyson and about twenty officers interrupted the ceremony. He walked right up to Eric and Nicole. "You are both under arrest for the murder of Frank Russo," he said with a smirk on his face as he watched his officers put handcuffs on the bride and groom. "You have the right to remain silent and anything you say can and will be used against you in the court of law."

"I'm going to make you pay for this," Eric growled. "You embarrassed me and my wife on our wedding day; you are the devil."

"Nothing personal Eric, but business is business," Detective Tyson said as he escorted the bride and groom out in handcuffs.

TO BE CONTINUED....

BOOKS BY GOOD2GO AUTHORS